Spring Break in Tampa with A Gangsta

By: Phoenixx Rose

Dream & Fantasy

"You sure about this shit?"

"Bitch, it's almost fifty stacks! Sage is on board with the shit. He already told me what to do and how to do it without it coming back to us."

"Fan, how many times have I told you about trusting these niggas out here? The plan is to get these niggas wrapped up, dope their asses up and steal their shit. How you know this nigga Sage ain't trying to set you up?"

"'Cause, I know Sage. We been hanging real close for a few months now, and things are starting to get serious with us. Sage has my back on this one, and I just need you to trust me on this too."

"Of course, I trust you. I don't trust Sage. How do you know his ass ain't trying to set you up? The nigga could be just like his punk ass brother."

"Ugh, Fan, you gotta let that shit go, for real. Sis, what happened between you and Life is ancient. I thought we moved on from that, and besides, what better way to get the nigga back for fucking you than to fuck him in the ass?"

"As much as I want revenge on his ass, I ain't trying to die for it. Fan, you know Life is crazy and ruthless as fuck. He won't hesitate to body you, me, Sage, or anybody else involved if he finds out we did this shit."

"Dream, just trust me on this. If I didn't think I could pull this shit off, I wouldn't do it. But Sage and I already discussed how to handle this shit. It's going to look like someone ran up on Sage, beat his ass, and robbed him. Life won't figure out that this was staged by us."

"I hope you're right. Just please think this shit through and make sure all your fucking corners are covered. I gotta get ready to go; Xavier is waiting for me."

"Who's Xavier?"

"Bitch, Xavier Thompson, the wide receiver for the Buccaneers. We've been chatting through IG for a week, and he's in town tonight."

"How much are you trying to get out of him?"

"He's known for being flashy and shit, and plus, I heard through one of his teammates that he always carries at least twenty stacks on him. So, you know me. I'm taking all of his shit."

"Okay. Well, I'm going to need your help to pull off my mission with Sage. Just call me once you're done with your date, and I can fill you in on the details."

I gave my sister a kiss before heading out of the door to go cash out on yet another rich ass nigga. Sliding into my brand-new Lexus snow white Genesis, I turned up the volume to Cardi B and Megan Thee Stallion's "WAP" and pulled out of the driveway. Singing the lyrics to my favorite song, I sped down I-4, headed to the Westin Hotel downtown.

Hitting damn near ninety, I weaved in and out of traffic in a hurry to get to my little boo thang. Xavier Thompson was one of the top paid athletes in the NFL, which meant he had big bank. After I had a little rendezvous with his teammate, Anthony Willis, before he got traded to the Broncos, Xavier jumped in my DM, wanting some play time, but little did he know, it was definitely going to cost him. He wasn't all that good-looking in the face, but he was sexy as fuck and better than that, his money was even sexier.

While my twin sister, Fantasy, ran game on dope boys, I was fixated on big dick, big money ballers. And Xavier was definitely easy prey. Niggas saw a pretty ass face with a sexy ass body and went crazy; they all wanted a slice of the pie. But if you knew how to play the game, you could make these niggas bend at your will. See, most girls looked at athletes, rappers and anybody with money and thought if they put the pussy on them real good, they'd get a ring and live happily ever after. Hell, some of these ditzy bitches would even go as far as trying to trap these niggas and get pregnant or some shit. But that was where they fucked up. Just like women were smart, so were these niggas, especially when it came to protecting their families, images, and most importantly, their money.

I was nothing like these thirsty ass hoes who had the game all fucked up. I wasn't looking for a husband, and I damn sure wasn't trying to have no baby. I made sure I went to my doctor every ninety days to get a shot in my ass. All I was chasing was a big ass bag. I didn't need a man to satisfy me. I took care of myself and paid my own bills by using what I got to make these niggas cum. And while I be fake moaning most of the time, the only thing that made me cum was the money I was cashing out.

Finally pulling up to the hotel, I valet parked and switched my ass in my black and gold Versace printed catsuit. My six-inch, open-toe platforms that showed off my freshly painted white toes clanked against the marble floors as I made my way to the receptionist's desk. Unlike ninety-five percent of American women who all had the same body shape, I was not about to get lost in the sauce, following the trend to inject my ass with silicone. I stood 5'7" and 120 pounds with natural, perky breasts, the perfect little apple ass, and Angelina Jolie naturally plump lips. From my sun-kissed, warm, olive skin tone, most people thought I was Brazilian or something, but I was Blasian, which was short for Black and Asian. I may not have had the big, round Nicki Minaj ass and peanut butter thick thighs, but I was as bad of a bitch as they came because I was pretty as fuck and smart as hell. I could hold a conversation with anyone on any topic, whether it was politics, sports or technology; I knew it all, and I used it to my advantage.

"Good evening, Ms. Walker. Your guest is waiting for your arrival in the executive suite." Alyssa, the receptionist, smiled at me as she slid my key across the counter. Reaching into my Birkin, I pulled out an envelope that contained a thousand dollars inside and winked at her as I walked away. Alyssa was my bitch. We went to high school together, and any chance we got, we would hang out and make some money together. She was the sole reason I made anyone I was hooking up with check in at this hotel. For one, it was beautiful with an amazing view, and two, this was Alyssa's hotel, and she had my back. I would call and tell her who I was meeting and when, and she would make sure the cameras were set up in the room before they checked in.

Xavier was already anxiously awaiting my arrival. As soon as I walked in, he was all over me, begging me to ride his ass like pony. And I gave him just what he wanted, plus something a little extra. After first giving him a strip tease and seductive lap dance, I had him right where I wanted him. Moving at the speed of lightning, I slipped GHB in his drink while he undressed himself and waited for him to down it before I fucked his ass unconscious. While he was out cold, I took everything he had in his safe — a Cuban link necklace, Cartier glasses, a Rolex, and sixty thousand in cash. Then, I hacked into his phone, logged into to his Amex account, and transferred twenty thousand dollars to my bank account and another ten thousand from his private account.

When I was done, I took a nice, hot shower to wash the smell of his basic ass sex off me and changed into my black Balenciaga mini dress and matching sneakers, applied my makeup, and brushed out my Brazilian bundles. Xavier was still out cold when I finished getting dressed, but before I left, I checked to make sure the recording from our sex scenes were downloaded on my phone. I sent a copy to my email and a snippet to Xavier's DM with a cute message attached. Lastly, I had to make sure I removed all of the hidden cameras before leaving the room. Stepping onto the elevator, I couldn't help but laugh at how dumb these niggas were — all over the chance to slip in some wet ass pussy. There was no doubt in my mind that Xavier would be confused as fuck whenever he woke up, but I didn't give a damn. Even if he did piece together the events from tonight, he would never tell a soul because it would do more damage to him than it ever could to me. The only thing he could do was consider himself stamped by the best. After all, my name was Dream for a reason; when they first laid their eyed on me, they couldn't help but fall into the sweetest trance, only to wake up to their worst fucking nightmare.

The Entitled Princess

Dior

I was having the most beautiful dream of a lifetime. I was on a gondola ride in Venice with the sexiest beast on the planet, Idris Elba. The sun was setting. We were sipping champagne and coming up on the Rialto Bridge when suddenly, a banner stretched down the center of the bridge with the question, 'Will you marry me?' I was just about to scream yes when a hard knock come at my door, sucking me out of the best part of my dream.

"Ugh! WHAT?!" I yelled out, pissed off that I was being awakened out of my sleep, and it was barely eight in the morning.

"Dior, get up, sweetheart. We have a family meeting in five," my daddy spoke from the other side of the door. I hated when he woke me up so early, especially with one of his bullshit meetings that was always pointless. Looking up at the ceiling, my mind wondered about what the reason was for a meeting this time. I was sure that whatever he wanted to talk about, had something to do with his stupid ass wife. My parents had split up when I was just three years old, and then she died when I fourteen, after being diagnosed with cervical cancer. Two years later, he had got married to Amora. She and I never had a great relationship because I felt like she was trying to be my mom. What made me hate her ass even more was that this bitch started interfering with the way he disciplined me and how much allowance he gave me. As soon as she started coming between me and my money, was the second I wanted to beat the shit out of her non-English, Colombian ass.

Me and my daddy, however, were super close. I'd always been daddy's little girl. Even after his witch of a wife had a son and a daughter; I still came first, and that shit would never change. Don't get it twisted, I loved my brother and sister with all my heart. It was their mother who could kiss the crack of my ass on a hot, summer day. My daddy meant the world to me, and although me and Amora never saw eye to eye, he always had my back whenever she'd come at him with some bullshit. But lately, things were starting to change, and it wasn't for my good either.

Agitatedly, I threw the covers back and got out of my comfortable, California King bed. I was still pissed off with my daddy for denying me a bomb ass trip to Cabos for Spring Break, so I wasn't trying to see his face right now. I slipped into my house slippers and dragged my feet to the bathroom to empty my bladder and brush my teeth. I took my time, walking slowly downstairs to the family room, where my daddy and Amora were sitting side by side, holding hands. I didn't know if my eyes were playing tricks on me or what, but it almost looked like Amora had been crying. Her face looked very weak and pale. I hoped like hell she wasn't sitting her ass up in this house with Covid. I kept my distance, just in case and stayed with my back leaning against the wall. My little brother, Ashton, and my sister, Amirah, were sitting on the other couch, looking just as pissed off as I was to be woken up so early.

"Okay, now that everyone is here and half-way awake, your mother and I have some news to share with everyone." My dad began to speak, and I knew by the seriousness in his voice that he wasn't on bullshit this time. Something was definitely wrong.

"Your mother and I have been keeping this quiet for quite some time now because for one, we wanted to make sure we had all the information correct before involving you guys. We didn't want you to get alarmed if it wasn't necessary. But we want you all to know that no matter what, we love you, and we are all going to get through this as a family, together."

"What's going on, daddy?" I had to interrupt because the theatrics were killing me. The way he was talking only led to two outcomes — he and Amora were getting a divorce, or we were going broke. And if it was the second outcome, someone should go ahead and pick out my casket right now.

"There really isn't an easy way to say this to you guys, but Amora has just been diagnosed with stage three cervical cancer."

When I heard the news, a very small part of me felt bad for Amora. This was the same cancer that took my mother away from me, and as much as I despised her ass at times, I didn't wish death on her. I really felt bad for my daddy and siblings. They loved and cared for Amora way more than I did, so I knew they were devastated. I, honestly, wasn't really moved all that much. Yeah, it was fucked up that she had cancer, but that was life. I wasn't going to sit there and try to squeeze out fake tears like my heart was broken, when it was what it was.

Ashton was obviously upset about learning the news of his mother's health because he rushed to her side, crying like today was her last day on earth or something. Amirah had a little bit more gangster in her. She acted more like her big sister. We lacked the ability to show emotions, and that was something my dad couldn't stand. But I couldn't help that I was strong individual, and I didn't allow every little thing going on to alter my mood or cause me to have a nervous breakdown.

I glanced over at Ashton and my dad comforting Amora, drowning in their tears. Amirah was on the other couch, staring one way, with a nonchalant look painted on her face. She and Amora had gotten into a little altercation a couple of days ago because she wanted to go to this camp for spring break, and Amora denied her. Maybe this very moment was the reason why, but you just never know when it came to Amora. She sheltered her kids way too much. They could barely play with the next-door neighbors without her lurking over their shoulders.

"Now, before everyone goes to thinking all crazy, the doctors have a solid plan in place that is eighty percent effective, if executed properly. Your mother can beat this thing, but we're going to need your strength and your help to get us through these tough weeks ahead of us. Some of the best oncologists in the U.S. are going to give your mother the best treatment possible, but we have to relocate to Fort Worth for a little while. It'll just be for a few weeks at a time, so that means we're going to need you, Dior," my dad looked towards me. I mean, sure, I was the oldest, but I didn't know a damn thing about looking after kids. Amirah was fifteen, and Ash had just turned fourteen, so I just assumed they could handle themselves.

"W-what do you mean, you're going to need me?"

"While Amora and I are in Fort Worth, I need you to look after your brother and sister. Estella will be here as well, but I'm depending on you, Button." I tried to contain my frustration, but I hated when he called me Button. It was such a stupid ass name, and it irritated me. That was what my mom used to call me. "I know you still have college and your own life to worry about, but I really need your help with this."

My eyes shifted from my brother to my sister and then back to my daddy. I nodded in agreeance, but it was only because of Ashton and Amirah. I damn sure wasn't happy about it, but I'd been in their shoes, and I'd only wished I had siblings to lean on when my mom went through this.

"So, with that being said, your mother and I came up with a plan for us all to spend some quality family time together before our first trip to Fort Worth in a few weeks. We're all leaving to go to Paris in two days to spend spring break there."

I immediately felt like someone had knocked the wind out of me when my dad announced that the entire family was going to Paris. Ash and Amirah screeched with excitement, but I was beyond pissed off. Just a few days ago, my daddy told me that he wasn't paying for my trip with my friends to Mexico, but yet, here he was, trying to take us all to Paris. At this point, I was livid.

"So, you can pay for a trip for four people to Paris, but I can't go to Cabo with my friends?" I spoke up with my hands crossed over my chest.

"Excuse me? What did you just say?" My dad shot an angry look in my direction.

"You heard me. Daddy, I just asked you to pay for my trip to Cabo so I could hang out with all of my friends, which would cost half as much as this family trip."

"I need to speak to you in private." He stood to his feet and pointed for me to exit out of the room. But my stubborn ass wouldn't budge.

"Why do we need to speak in private? We can talk right here."

"Dior Amelia Carmichael, take your little ass out of this room right now."

"But da—"

"I SAID NOW!" The thunderous roar in his voice made everyone in the room damn near jump out of their drawers. My father rarely raised his voice to me, but when he did, I knew I pushed his limit. I couldn't even lie, when he got angry like this, it kind of scared the shit out of me a little. My daddy was what I liked to call a gentle giant, but when he got pissed, everyone had better get the hell out of his way.

He was right on my heels when I turned to leave out of the room. As soon as I rounded the corner to the kitchen, my dad grabbed me by the forearm, forcefully sitting me down on the barstool. I probably should have been scared to death, but I wasn't. I was just as pissed off as he was.

"What is your fucking problem, Dior?"

"My problem? My problem is you, daddy! You make me feel like I don't matter as much to you as your wife and kids."

"So, because I won't give you twenty thousand dollars to blow for one damn week, I'm treating you different? Who pays for your tuition? Who just gifted you a G-Wagon because you said you were tired of riding around in your Lexus? Who allowed your grown, twenty-one-year-old ass to continue living in this house, walking around, doing whatever you please? Anything you need or want, I provide for you without hesitation, so how dare you sit here in my face and say some shit like this to me?"

"Because every single day, it's like she's influencing you to back away from me. I don't get the allowance that you used to give me anymore, and everything I do or ask for is becoming a problem now. But when your wife wants something, you jump to get it done."

"Did you not hear what I just told everyone about Amora? She's battling the very cancer that took your mother away from us, and yet you can stand here without a caring bone in your body, complaining about something that you didn't get. How could you be so selfish, Dior? I didn't raise you to be this way."

"I do feel bad that she's sick, daddy, but what do you want me to do about it? I can't help that I don't show my emotions."

"You don't care about nothing or no one but yourself, and that's what breaks my heart. I give you everything in this world, and this is the repayment I get? This trip was for us to enjoy each other's company as a family before Amora's condition takes a turn for the worse. Can't you see that?" My dad's voice lowered to almost a tremble, and his eyes glistened as if he were about to cry. Much like myself, my dad was super strong and brave. He tried his best to keep his emotions in check, but I guess this was a little too overwhelming.

"Daddy, I'm sorry." The last thing I wanted to do was hurt my daddy. I may not have cared much for his wife, but I hated it when my daddy was upset with me.

"Dior, you are my first born, my pride and joy. I would move heaven and hell for you, baby. I know it's been hard on you growing up without your own mother, and I'm responsible for you being so spoiled because I just wanted you to feel that you weren't any less important in my life. But you're a grown woman now, and whether you want to accept it or not, Amora is my wife and the number one woman in my life. But I need you to know that I will never, never love you any less than I did the moment you were born."

Hearing my dad tell me Amora was his number one felt like a million knives stabbing me in the heart. My throat tightened, restricting my airflow, and I felt like I was about to pass out. I knew I shouldn't have been mad, but I couldn't help it. I didn't want anyone stepping in front of me when it came to my daddy. That was why I hated Amora so much. It wasn't because she mistreated me or anything. It was because I knew I would no longer have my daddy all to myself. And that hurt like hell.

Bishop

Standing outside of my cousin's funeral home, I anxiously waited for Life to get his ass over here. I hated being around this place with dead ass bodies lying around, some of them even being burned and shit. Since I was the only one here, I'd be damned if I stepped inside of that bitch by myself. I was creeped out enough just standing on the outside of this building. I pulled out a pre-rolled joint and took a few hits to calm my nerves before Life pulled up because when that nigga heard the news I was about to lay on his ass, all hell was going to break loose.

Life was my best friend, and that motherfucker made big shit pop. We both grew up together in Temple Terrace, where we were mostly raised by our grandmothers. We were more than just friends; we treated each other more like brothers. Even though I was older, Life was always the smarter, more calculated one. I was known as the muscle, the nigga that whopped ass first and took names later. Life, on the other hand, was quiet and low-key. See, niggas in the streets were scared of me because they knew how I was coming. But Life, you never knew what to expect. You cross him, that nigga made you pay in the worst ways you could ever think of and go home and sleep like a newborn baby. Together, we ran the whole city of Tampa, pushing more weight throughout the city than you could keep up with.

Our crew was small because Life didn't trust a single soul. His motto was, the larger the crew, the greedier motherfuckers got, and sooner than later, everyone falls. We didn't sell to any random motherfucker, and only two people were responsible for the pickups and drop-offs. Everything else was handled by Life. My job was to keep accountability of everything moving in and out. But last night, when one of our most trusted movers who also happened to be Life's baby cousin, Sage, showed up with a busted nose and a swollen eye like he'd just gone twelve rounds with Mayweather, I knew some major shit was about to go down. And the worst of it all was that whoever ran down on Sage, took everything he was transporting.

Twenty minutes later, Life's all black Rolls-Royce Cullinan pulled up in the parking lot. The windows on that motherfucker were so dark, I don't think he could see from the inside. Now, I was far from a bitch, but as soon as Life stepped out of his truck, my heart skipped a beat because I knew this nigga was about to snap when he found out what happened to his little cousin. Sage was more than just a blood relative to Life; he treated the nigga like his little brother, taking him under his wings and showing him how to be a man. They even referred to each other as brothers. That's how close they were. Life always felt the need to protect Sage because he looked up to him, so I knew for a fact this shit wasn't going to go over smoothly. However, I was more nervous for Sage because both myself and Life preached to him constantly about rolling in these streets carelessly. Now, he was going to have to explain all of this shit to his brother and hope he didn't get a second ass whooping.

"Fuck you standing out here for?" Life questioned as he walked up to me. If you weren't from Tampa, you would think Life was just some thug ass nigga with a lot of money because he was just 5'6" and roughly 150 pounds, give or take. The nigga was a short ass, light-skinned version of that comedian Kevin Hart, just a couple inches taller. At first glance, you would think Life was some Mickey Mouse ass nigga, but put him up against anybody, and he'd rock their ass. For a little nigga, Life was nice with his hands, like a modern-day Holyfield. Not to mention, he damn sure wasn't afraid to body any motherfucker.

"Nigga, you know I hate going in this bitch by myself."

"Tsk. Scary ass. So, what happened?" Life asked, making his way down the hall to his office, taking a seat behind the desk.

"I don't know why every time you go out of town some shit always pops off. Niggas be getting real relaxed when you ain't around."

"I can see that. But enough of the small talk. What's the word?"
I hesitated a minute before taking a deep breath and responding. "Sage got jacked last night."

"The fuck you mean he got jacked? Why the fuck ain't nobody call me?" Life rose to his feet in fury. Two things that nigga didn't play about was his family and his business. You fucked with either one, and the likelihood of you living to tell the story were slim to none.

"He didn't tell me shit till this morning when I rolled up on him to pick up the money. The nigga face look like Martin when he fought Hitman. I hit you up as soon as he told me what happened."

"Who the fuck was it and how much they take?" Life's entire face turned bright red. That was how pissed off he was, pacing the floor back and forth with clenched fists.

"He said he don't know. But the nigga had a honey bun on him."

"FUCK!" Losing his cool, Life knocked everything on his deck to the floor in one swipe, including the brand new three thousand Apple iMac he just bought last week. "Where is he? Where the fuck is Sage at?"

"He's at the crib."

"Tell that nigga to get the fuck down here right now!"

A whole hour had passed, and that nigga Life was still fuming at the mouth when Sage finally made it to the funeral home. I could tell by his posture and the look in his eyes that he was scared shitless to face his big brother. Personally, the nigga's whole story sounded bogus as fuck to me, but I just stayed quiet and let Life handle this shit.

"Nigga, don't walk in here looking all slump and shit. What the fuck happened?" Life started barking at Sage before he could even take a seat.

"I don't know what happened, bro. I was on my way to make the drop when I got a call from one of our regulars who wanted some work. I was right around the corner and figured I had time to handle that real quick. Then, next thing I know, some bitches ran down on me. I couldn't see shit."

"Clearly." Life pointed out Sage's half-shut eye. "Sage, you fucking know better than that shit. You got work or money on you, you know not to stop for any fucking thing! Not even to piss! The fuck was you thinking?"

"Bro, it was for Stan. You know that nigga breaks major bread with on us every single time. I couldn't turn it down."

"I wouldn't give a fuck if that nigga was buying a million dollars' worth of work. Nigga, you could have got fucked up worse than what your fucking eye look like. And judging by the way you can't even fucking look me in my eyes, lets me know something else went down. Is there something else you need to tell me? 'Cause now is your only fucking chance."

"No. Life, I'm being real with you."

Life's eyes shifted from Sage to me and then back to Sage. When he did that, the wheels in his heads were starting to turn, and that was when the nigga was really ready to pop off. He closed his eyes and took a deep breath before taking a seat back behind his desk. He was quiet for a little too long, which made me worry for Sage.

"Yo, Bishop. Go holla at Stan and find out what that nigga know, and see what the word on the street is."

"Say less."

"Sage, you better pray like a motherfucker I don't find out you lying to me. 'Cause brother or not, I'll stretch your ass my damn self."

I wasted no time in getting my ass the fuck up out of there. Whatever was about to go down between those two brothers, I ain't want no parts of it. This wasn't the first time Sage and Life had issues, but this was the maddest Life had ever been because a good chunk of his money was unaccounted for. To Life, that was the ultimate betrayal, and if Sage wasn't being truthful, there wasn't no telling what the fuck was gonna happen.

<h1 style="text-align:center">Spring Break Dupe</h1>

<h3 style="text-align:center">Dior</h3>

"Bitch, it's spring break! You gotta come kick it with us out here. I haven't seen your ass since Thanksgiving."

"Fan, you have no idea how much more I would enjoy my spring break vacation if I were with yah'll than be stuck in Paris with everyone else. But there is no way my daddy is going to go for it. You should have seen him. He damn near chopped my head off when I questioned him about why I couldn't go to Cabo."

"But that's different. You were trying to go to Cabo with just friends; we're your family, your favorite cousins at that, and not to mention Uncle Quincy's favorite nieces. I know for sure he will be cool with you coming to hang with us. I'm telling you, Dior, it's going to be super lit in Tampa for spring break. All week long, there's going to be party after party with all types of niggas. Trust me, you cannot miss this."

"You're making it so hard to say no, cousin. But I really don't think my dad is going to say yes. He's already chewed me a new ass for being "ungrateful", as he calls it. I just don't know." Laying across my bed, I stared at the ceiling, feeling lost and hopeless. Usually, I was able to talk my daddy into saying yes to anything that I wanted, but now that he allowed his dumb ass wife come in and control everything, I feel so left out and thrown to the side. Instead of being daddy's princess and him promising to always take care of me, I'd become the red-headed stepchild that no one wanted. It was almost like this wasn't even my real family anymore, and I no longer had a place in this house.

"Okay, well how about this; I'll call Uncle Quincy and ask him myself. How could he say no to his little Fanny-Fan?"

"If he can say no to me, he can definitely say no to you. But if you think you can pull it out of him, by all means, go for it, boo."

"Oh, girl, you haven't seen my Academy Award winning performance before, have you? I can guarantee, in ten minutes, he's going to come in your room and say you can come out to Tampa. Just watch the master work, and I'll text you in a few. Pack your bags, bitch, 'cause you're coming."

I semi believed that Fantasy could get through to my dad, but I damn sure wasn't holding my breath for it. This man was not the same man he was a few years ago, and I was starting to hate that shit more and more every single day. It killed me that my dad could let this foreign ass, half-English speaking, Gisele Bündchen wannabe bitch just come into my house and take shit over. Things were perfect the way they were before she sank her venom into my dad and made it all about her and her kids. As much as my dad wanted to turn a blind eye, he knew this bitch saw him as a meal ticket, and she cashed in. But I'll be damned if she was going to exclude me out of my father's life and fortune. I'd kill that money-hungry bitch myself before I ever let that happen.

About an hour had passed by, and I'd dozed off to sleep when I heard a knock come at my door. I didn't even bother to open my eyes to see who it was because only two people knocked and let themselves into my room — my dad and Amirah. But the shuffling of heavy feet was a dead giveaway that it was my dad.

"Dior? Baby girl, get up for a second. I need to have a conversation with you." He gently shook me by the shoulder as he sat on the side of my bed.

"What's up, daddy?"

"Well, I just got off the phone with your cousin, Fanny. I'm sure you already knew about that, though."

"She called, wanting me to come spend the spring break

holiday with them in Tampa, but I told her we were going to Paris. I didn't tell her to call you."

"I know. And I gave it some thought and spoke to Amora about it as well."

"Daddy, why do you have to talk to her about everything? What does she have to do with this conversation?"

"Because she's my wife, Dior. Did we not just talk about this the other day? You know, I really don't get what your anger is towards her. She's never mistreated you, never disrespected you in the least. All she's ever tried to do was be part of your life, and you continue to push her away. Why?"

"I don't push her away. I just…" I sighed heavily, not even wanting to go back down this road again with my dad because he would always find a way to turn things around on me. I was so over this shit. "I just don't want to talk about it anymore."

"Anyway, Amora and I would both really love it if you came along with us to Paris. I miss my baby girl, and I want us to be able to spend time together like we used to. But Amora did remind me that you're a young adult, and spring break is a very important time for you kids to take a break from school and enjoy life with your friends. So, with that being said, if you would like to go to Tampa with your cousins, you may go."

"Really, daddy?" My face instantly lit up like a Christmas tree. Paris would be nice, but Tampa seemed more of my speed, and I wouldn't have to worry about my dad or Amora breathing down my neck the entire time.

"But, I will be booking your room for you, so I know you're staying in a safe and well secured place, and there will be a cap on your bank account so that you don't go crazy out there."

"A cap? Well, what's my limit?"

"Twenty-five hundred."

"WHAT?! Daddy, are you serious? This is spring break we're

talking about. What am I supposed to do with twenty-five hundred dollars?" I couldn't believe that this man, who made nearly a million dollars a month, maybe more, just tried my fucking life with a lousy twenty-five hundred dollars. That was the kind of money I'd spend in a day just getting my hair, nails, and toes done.

"Most college students your age could have an amazing time for spring break with half that amount. I'm paying for your flight, a rental car, and hotel. What more do you want from me, Dior?"

"But daddy, I need clothes to take with me. I need to get my hair done, I need shopping money and food. Come on, daddy, this is not fair."

"Fair? No, what's not fair is that you're a grown ass woman who's never wanted for anything your entire life and who's been treated like a princess since the day you were born. You can be so entitled and selfish. I work my ass off to make sure this family is taken care of the best I can. I pay for your tuition, that expensive car you have sitting in the driveway, along with your ridiculous spending habits, and this is how you come at me?"

By the look on my daddy's face, I knew I was hurting his feelings, and I really wasn't trying to. I knew a lot of times, I did feel entitled, but it was only because that was the way he raised me. Anything I asked for, my dad didn't hesitate to give it to me. This was the lifestyle I was accustomed to, and it wasn't easy to try and be selfless and humble when I'd never had to. It was like taking a house dog and releasing it to the woods, expecting it to survive. But I knew that if I was ever going to find myself back in my father's good graces and finally start getting what I wanted, I had no choice but to swallow my pride and attempt to be more sensitive.

"Okay, okay. Daddy, I'm sorry. I didn't mean to upset you. I appreciate you allowing me to go to Tampa for the week."

"Baby girl, I don't mean to be so hard on you, but I just need you to really grasp the fact that I have more than just you to take care of. But as long as there is breath in my body, I'll never let you go without. I love you, sweetheart."

"I love you too, daddy. I'm sorry." I wrapped my arms around my daddy's neck, squeezing him tightly and planted a kiss on his cheek. I was still very much pissed off about that lousy twenty-five hundred dollars, but I remembered I still had access to my dad's safe at his office downtown, and I knew for a fact he kept at least fifty stacks locked up. If he wasn't going to willingly give me what I deserved, then he left me no other option but to just take it.

Sneaking Around

Dream

Standing in the shower, letting the hot water beat against my back, I thought about how dazed and confused Xavier must have been when he woke up to an empty hotel room with all of his expensive shit gone. It was so funny how dumb these niggas could be, all for the sake of getting some pussy. They let this pretty ass face fool them every single time. And tonight was going to be the same thing with Kasey Richmond, one of Tampa's most affluent and successful real estate developers. His company recently finished building twenty-six homes in the Davis Islands community. Every home was no less than eight hundred thousand dollars, and they just closed on the final one. I knew his pockets were heavily packed, and I couldn't wait to get my hands on some of that cash.

Kasey was in his late fifties but extremely handsome and well-fit. He reminded me of that wrestler turned actor, The Rock. He aged very gracefully. Of course, he was married with children around the same age as me, but none of that shit mattered to me. All I saw was dollar signs, and it only took for me to like a few of his pictures on Instagram before he was in my inbox flirting. And tonight, I was going to make sure his wildest dreams came true because I was coming to collect a big ass bag.

I was in the shower so long, trying to scheme up the perfect plan for tonight, the water was starting to get lukewarm, so I quickly cleaned my ass before the water got too cold. As soon as I stepped out of the shower, I heard the front door to our apartment close. I could have sworn I locked the damn door before getting in the shower, and there was no way Fantasy was back from the airport already. It could have just been our housekeeper, Jess, but just to be on the safe side, I grabbed my Tiffany Blue .380 and tiptoed down the hall. I didn't even have time to dry the excess water from my body, but I was ready to send a bitch the meet their maker if someone was stupid enough to break in on me. Just as I rounded the corner from the kitchen, I spotted Sage's stupid ass, peeking through my sister's bedroom door.

"Sage! What the fuck are you doing, and how did you get in here?" I pointed my straight at his face.

"Whoa! Damn, girl, relax. I was just looking for Fantasy." He jumped back with both hands up in the air, like I was a police officer, ready to let off rounds in his ass.

"You ever heard of ringing the fucking doorbell instead of just letting yourself in? I almost shot your dumb ass."

"I apologize. I didn't know you were here."

"Whatever. Fantasy ain't even here. She's at the airport, picking up my cousin."

"Is that right?" He glanced at my body up and down seductively before walking towards me. "So that means we got some time to ourselves then, huh?"

"Uh, wrong. We ain't got shit together." I held my hand up as soon as he got up close to my face, trying to grab me.

"Really? You gon' act like that now, baby?"

"You damn straight. Aren't you and my sister in a so-called relationship now?"

"Bae, you know how gullible your Fantasy is. She'll believe anything that comes out of my mouth, and you know that was the only way I could get her to agree to get the money from Life."

"I agreed to you getting close to my sister, but I didn't expect for you to make the bitch fall in love with you. How you go from fucking me to fucking my sister and expect to still hit this? I don't think so." I rolled my eyes and proceeded to head back into my room when he grabbed ahold of my towel, wrapping his arms around my waist. The hairs from his thick, Rick Ross beard tickled my shoulder as his lips pecked at my skin.

"Don't even try to act like what I got going on with Fan bothers you. You knew how much a nigga was feeling you from day one, but then you went and fucked on my brother. And look where that shit got you. A baby and a boot to the curb."

"Fuck you, Sage!" I elbowed him as hard as I could in the sternum.

"Aight, aight. I'm sorry, baby. I didn't mean that. But don't act like we both ain't did some foul shit to each other. Shit, you really think I let you and Fan kick my ass like this for nothing? I did this for you, bae."

"And what the fuck are we supposed to do with fifty thousand, Sage? That ain't gonna get us nowhere."

"But it's a start. Plus, I got plenty of connections in Atlanta that'll help me get my own operation started. If you trust me and love me like you said you did, just give me some time, and we can make this shit work."

"What about Fantasy?"

"What about her? She ain't who I want, and you know that. It's you, bae. So, stop acting all stuck up and shit with me. You know that stank ass attitude of yours only turns me on even more." Slipping his hand down my back and under my towel, he found my honey hole and began stroking it slowly. "I miss that sweet ass pussy so much, bae."

"Oh, really? Show me how much you missed it."

Turning me around, he snatched my towel from around me and scooped me up. Sage reminded me so much of Life; they were both red bones, tatted up, and sexy as fuck. But Sage looked more like a high school, wannabe gangsta because he was so skinny, but he held his own quite well. I knew he was crazy in love with me and willing to do whatever I said, including stealing from his own blood. But the sad truth of the matter was that nothing he could do or say would ever make him better than Life in my eyes. That was where my heart lied; Sage was just a means to get closer to who I really craved.

Sitting me down on the kitchen island, Sage kissed me passionately while his fingers continued to work my middle, and all I could think of was Life and the way he used to send my body into an electric shock every single time he touched me. Out of all the niggas I'd been with, no one on this earth could ever hold a candle to Life and the things he did to me. He could look at me, and my pussy would instantly get wet, and every time we fucked and he told me to cum, my body responded within seconds. That's the kind of power he had over me, and I wanted my baby back.

I pretended to be so into Sage as he ate my pussy out. Moaning while gripping his head, I couldn't stop thinking about Life. His face was all I saw when I closed my eyes, and I pictured it being him eating me out instead of Sage. I was so deep in thought, focused on Life, that I damn near called his name out loud, but I caught myself before I let it slip. He made my pussy cum in just the nick of time as I happened to look over at the small monitor on the counter and saw Fantasy's car pulling up. I pushed his ass off me and gave him a quick peck on the lips before racing back in my room and turning the shower back on as if I had been in there the whole time when she walked in. I knew what Sage and I were doing was dead wrong, but I wasn't trying to intentionally hurt my sister. I loved her with all of my heart, but when it came down to it, I was only using Sage to get Life back. I just hoped Fantasy could understand where I was coming from.

Time to Turn Up

Dior

Finally! I was a free woman. No one hovering over my shoulder and I was able to do whatever the fuck I wanted to do. And I planned on turning all the way up while I was in Tampa. My dad had booked a bad ass suite for me and my cousins at the Westin, and I couldn't wait to get the party started. As soon as I landed, Fantasy picked me up at the airport. My rental was going to be delivered at the hotel later on, and Dream had some important business to tend to, so while she was out, Fantasy showed me all the hot spots of the city. I was all but too excited to turn this place upside down. I wanted to get white girl wasted and find a sexy ass nigga to bang my brains out all fucking week long.

It was late as hell when Dream had finally made it back home from whatever she was doing, so we all just crashed at the hotel and decided to kick things off first thing in the morning. Fantasy and Dream were the only girl cousins I had on my daddy's side. Their father was my dad's older brother, and rumor had it, he was heavy in the streets, selling drugs and whatnot. Unfortunately, he was killed when the girls were twelve, and their mother was deemed unfit to raise them, so they had to go into foster care. We lost touch for a little while until they turned seventeen and left foster care to take their lives into their own hands. I wasn't exactly sure what all they were doing to make a living, but they obviously were living the good life, if you asked me.

After we had breakfast, we all got dressed in our cute little bikinis and booty shorts to head to the Ben T. Davis beach.

Supposedly, this was the most popular beach in the entire city, and it was especially lit during spring break time. I was just ready to get in these streets and see what these Tampa boys were all about. And judging by the stares and whistling as we stepped down the streets, things were most definitely about to get heated around here.

We weren't even on the beach for ten minutes before we had a group of football players from USF sending up shots of tequila. They were fine as fuck, but I wasn't really trying to be tied down with some hormonal, young college boys. I wanted to get next to some grown ass men with deep ass pockets. These college boys were great to hang out with for some laughs and free drinks, but that was all. Apparently, my cousins and I had a lot in common when it came to the type of men we were looking for because after we ditched the college boys, Dream and I were in hot pursuit of the high-end ballers, while Fantasy was scoping for the dread-headed gangsters with gold teeth. I loved both of my cousins to death, and even though they were identical twins, they definitely had opposing personalities. Dream was more of the boujee, high-class twin, and Fantasy was a little immature and wild. But they had each other's backs, no matter what, and they knew how to party.

Fantasy wasn't lying when she told me over the phone that there were going to be fine ass boys all over the place. So far, I hadn't seen not a single broke, busted bum. Still, I hadn't spotted one person that made my stomach tighten or made my heart skip a beat. Dream had eased away from us after some rich, fly ass white boy grabbed her attention, and before I could turn around, some rapper looking dude was whisking Fantasy away, leaving me all by myself. So, I made my way over to the bar to get another drink. I was so busy looking down, checking my phone, I wasn't even looking at what was in front of me until it felt like I had run into a brick wall.

"Oh, shit! My bad, I didn't see you." I looked up and saw that I had bumped into the most gorgeous man I had seen in my lifetime. He was a little short but fine as fuck with tattoos from his neck down to his legs. His mouth was iced out in a platinum grill that hid behind the most beautiful, plump, pink lips. My mind instantly imagined how soft they would feel kissing every part of my body. But the way he frowned up at me let me know he wasn't too happy that I had spilled his drink.

"If your head wasn't in your damn phone, you'd see where the fuck you were going."

"You ain't gotta be so fucking rude. I said I was sorry."

"Don't be sorry, bitch, be fucking careful."

"Bitch? Nigga, who the fuck you think you're talking to? I ain't seen a bitch around until I bumped into you, with your rude, disrespectful ass."

"I see you ain't from around here 'cause you obviously don't know who the fuck you talking to. So, I'll give your Nicki Minaj wannabe ass a pass this time. But you better tread lightly, 'cause the next time, I won't be so fucking nice."

"Whatever." I rolled my eyes and stomped over to the bar. I had planned on getting myself a dirty martini, but that rude motherfucker had just fucked up my entire mood. I needed something hard and stiff to take the edge off.

"Hey, mami. What can I get you?" a young, Spanish chick asked as I sat down on the barstool.

"Something hard with no chaser."

"Oooh. The day starting off bad already? Spring Break is just beginning."

"I know, and some stupid ass bastard put a huge damper on my mood before I could actually start to enjoy my time out here."

"I can see," she said, pouring me a nice shot of Don Julio. "Where you from, sweetie?"

"Texas. I'm just here with my cousins for the spring break week."

"You know, I saw that guy who ruffled your feathers a minute ago. Since you're not from around here, I'd steer clear of him if I were you. Trust me, mami, he's nobody you want to cross."

"Who is he?"

"Let's just say, the city belongs to him, and he's one ruthless son of a bitch. Just be careful, okay?"

I tried to forget about what had transpired between me and that animal, but for some reason, I was intrigued a little bit. Even though he was rude as fuck and a total asshole when it wasn't even necessary, he gave me that feeling I'd been searching for since I got to Tampa — someone to make my stomach tighten and make my heart skip a beat. The second I looked into his eyes, I got that feeling, but it immediately disappeared when he disrespected me. He was fine and beautiful as fuck, but I wasn't about to let nobody come as me sideways, no matter who they were; my daddy taught me better than that. But, if I ever ran across him again while I was out here and he apologized, I probably wouldn't mind seeing if his dick matched his attitude.

Life

Gawk. Gawk. Gawk.

I sat reclined in my truck, checking the messages on my phone while my bitch, Golden, gave me some sloppy top. I really wasn't in the mood to deal with her ass, but after that dumb ass hoe rubbed me the wrong way at the beach earlier, I needed a release, and my bitch was on call twenty-four seven. Me and Golden had been kicking it for a couple years, but it was nothing serious — at least not to me. I knew she wanted a nigga to make a commitment to her, but the only thing I was committed to was being a father to my son and making money. I ain't have time to be no boyfriend or nothing else to these hoes.

While I should have been concentrating on Golden, I couldn't stop thinking about that bold ass bitch that spilled my fucking drink. Even though she pissed me off and I had to check her ass real quick, I couldn't deny how beautiful she was. And she was bad as fuck too — milk chocolate skin, big ass titties, small waist with a fat ass and thick thighs, and a gorgeous ass, innocent looking face. But that mouth. Shorty had a slick ass mouth on her, and I was not the type of nigga to just let anyone pop off on me, male or female. I was quick to chin check any bitch who came at me on some disrespectful shit. But there was something about this bitch that got to me, and I wanted to see who the fuck she was and what that mouth really do.

Gawk. Gawk. Gawk.

"You like that shit, bae?" Golden asked, coming up for some

air and fucking up my train of thought.

"Shut the fuck up and keep sucking. You 'bout to fuck a nigga nut up." I forced her head back down, shoving all eleven inches of dick in her mouth till she started choking. That thick bitch from the club had a nigga head all fucked up. Golden wasn't even doing shit for me right now. As fire as her head was, the only thing I could think about was the slick mouth bitch, with her pretty ass lips wrapped around my dick.

Closing my eyes, I tried to relax and focus on busting this nut when my phone starting ringing. Any other time, I would have ignored it, but since Golden wasn't really doing shit for me anyway, I happily answered.

"Yo."

"Life, your presence is needed at the restaurant, cuz."

"Say less. I'm on my way." I hung up and quickly pushed Golden off me. "Get up. I gotta roll."

"W-what? Now?"

"Yeah, now. I got shit to handle." Stuffing my dick back in my pants and fixing my clothes, I could feel Golden's cold ass eyes staring back at me, but she knew better than to question me.

"When am I going to be able to see you again?"

"I don't know. I'll hit you up, though."

"Can I at least get a kiss this time?"

"You know better than that. Make sure you grab all your shit. I gotta roll."

Golden snatched up all her shit and got out of my truck without even saying bye. I knew she was pissed off, but I really didn't give a fuck. She, of all people, should know by now that I had no filter or feelings for no bitch. I kept it real from the jump about what this was, and if she ain't like it, she knew where the fucking door was.

She had barely shut the door all the way before I sped off out of her apartment complex, headed towards my restaurant. I'd just recently opened a soul food restaurant with my grandmother as the head cook. I also owned a hookah lounge and funeral home, but that was just the tip of the iceberg. I was the city's biggest kingpin, running weight all across the state. Nobody could fuck with me when it came down to the type of products I was putting in the streets, and if any bitch ass nigga ever thought about trying to step on my turf, they paid for it with their lives. When it came to my money, my business and my family, I'd drop anybody. I was feared but mostly respected in the city 'cause everybody knew I was not the motherfucker to fuck with.

Twenty minutes later, I was pulling up into back parking lot of the restaurant when I spotted the delivery truck that was carrying both food and what was supposed to be twenty kilos of cocaine from my main supplier out of Texas that should have been here yesterday. So, I knew something was definitely wrong. Grabbing my Glock out of the glove compartment, I double checked to make sure one was in the chamber and tucked it behind my back before making my way inside to see what the fuck was going on.

Passing through the kitchen, I went straight to my padded, soundproof office, where the delivery man was sitting in a chair looking scared as fuck with Bishop and Sage standing on the side of him. I made sure the door was locked when I closed it and cautiously walked towards them to see what the fuck was going on. I already had Sage to deal with after he let some weak ass bitches jack his dumb ass, and now I had a feeling I was going to have to deal with some more bullshit. My eyes shifted from Bishop to Sage before I said anything.

"What happened?"

"Two keys missing from the shipment. Rocky Balboa over here tried to throw down with Sage and make a break for it before I stopped him," Bishop spoke first. I glanced over at Sage and noticed his nose bleeding a little bit. All I could do was shake my head in disappointment. Twice within a matter of days, this nigga got his ass whopped. Shit was embarrassing as fuck.

"You straight?" I asked Sage, not even really giving a fuck if he was okay or not because his bullshit was beginning to work on my fucking nerves.

"I'm cool, bro."

"So, where the fuck my dope at?" I asked the delivery boy.

"Eh, mi no hablo inglés." He threw his hands in the air as if he didn't understand what the fuck I was saying, which only insulted my intelligence.

Without second guessing, I whacked that motherfucker so hard in his mouth, he damn near flew out of the chair.

"Don't fucking insult me, motherfucker. So, since you claim you don't speak no motherfucking English, ¿donde esta mi mierda?"

"I don't know!"

"Oh, wow. He speaks English. What a miracle. Let me tell you something, motherfucker. I ain't got all day to sit here and go back and forth with you. I don't even have five minutes. And right now, you fucking with my money and my time, which I don't fucking appreciate. Now," I took my gun out and pointed it at his dick. "This is my last fucking time asking you, where the fuck is my shit?"

"I didn't do anything."

"Wrong answer, motherfucker." I didn't even hesitate to pull the trigger, putting a hole right in his dick. Naturally, he screamed at the top of his lungs like a little bitch. I was done wasting my time on this shit.

"That's for hitting my brother and lying to me, bitch ass nigga. Bishop, take care of this motherfucker."

"Say less."

"Sage, come take a walk with me."

I left Bishop to handle that motherfucker while I took Sage outside to holla at him about what the fuck had been going on with him lately. I could tell when this nigga was up to some shit, and right now, something was definitely not right. Sage was my blood, and I had a soft spot for him 'cause he always looked up to me, but my trust in him was starting to dwindle every single day. I made a promise to my grandmother that I would always look after him, but if I found out that this nigga was going against me, in hell she shall lift up his motherfucking eyes.

"What the fuck is going on with you, Sage?"

"What you mean? I'm just out here handling business."

"Handling business? Nigga, every time I turn around, you getting your ass kicked on every corner. I taught you better than that shit. Is there anything I need to know? 'Cause now is your fucking chance to let me know what's up."

"Man, that motherfucker in there blindsided me when I asked him where the missing keys were. All I been doing is busting my ass for you, and right now, I feel like you trying to question me or some shit."

"I ain't trying to do shit, nigga, I am questioning you. You think I don't see you, Sage? Nigga, you been moving weird as fuck lately, and then you get jacked for fifty stacks and don't even call me? You damn right I'm questioning you. Sage, you know I got your back, and anything you need, I would give it to you if you just ask. But the last thing you need to be doing is sneaking behind my fucking back. So, tell me right now, what the fuck is up?"

I could tell by the way he shifted his weight from one side to the other and could barely look me in the face, something was on his mind. All I could do was pray that he didn't orchestrate that bullshit jacking because if he did, I promise, this shit wasn't going to end well.

"Ain't shit going on, Life. I just feel like I don't get the recognition from you that I deserve. I feel like you and Bishop underestimate me and treat me like a fucking kid."

"You for real right now? I'm the motherfucker that put you on game, nigga. I trust you to handle my money and products, and I make sure you have everything you need. The only reason I keep you close is because I made a promise to grandma that I would never let shit happen to you. I know you, Sage, better than you know your fucking self, and I know you can be easily persuaded, and that shit will get you killed."

"I'm just saying, bro, I'm constantly in your light, and niggas think I can't hold my own. I just want to show you that I can handle business just like you."

"Hmm. Is that right? We'll see about that. But for now, go help Bishop get that shit cleaned up, and we'll talk later."

"Aight."

Something in my heart was telling me that Sage wasn't keeping it all the way real with me. He, of all people, should've known that I hated a fucking liar, and I hated a snake ass motherfucker.

I wasn't going to stop until I got down to the bottom of this shit, but right now, I had some other shit to deal with. There were two keys of coke missing from my shipment, and I needed to know where the fuck it was and who the fuck was responsible for taking my shit. Pulling out my phone, I dialed my supplier, who hired this stupid ass delivery man to let him know what was up.

"Life, what's up, my brother?" he answered on the second ring.

"We got a problem. Two keys were missing out of the shipment."

"Are you fucking kidding me?"

"I kid you not."

"Fuck! Listen, Life, I'll take the hit on this one. I left for a trip to Paris before making sure everything was straight. But don't worry, I'll get to the bottom of this shit."

"Cool. You might want to find someone else to pick up your payment 'cause your delivery boy is about to take a permanent dirt nap."

"I'll get something arranged, and then I'll call you back to let you know."

"Cool."

Meeting Again

Dior

"Bitch, we about to turn this bitch up! Cousin, are you ready to see how we get down in the FLA?" After downing three shots of tequila, Fantasy was already hyped for the club tonight. Dressed in a mini black halter dress that barely covered her ass, she was looking fine as well, and her makeup was immaculate with the deepest red lipstick that made her lips extra sexy. Wearing her hair slicked back in a thirty-inch straight ponytail, Fantasy was definitely dressed to kill tonight.

"Hell yeah. I'm ready to shake some ass and find some big ass dick to bounce on," I replied, standing in the mirror, applying my ginger-colored Kylie Cosmetics lipstick.

"Bitch, you're still a fucking virgin? How are you planning on taking some big dick?"

"Excuse me? Bitch, don't come for my sex life, okay? I have had sex before," I lied confidently, knowing damn well I had never taken a dick of any kind before in my life. I had come close once before but never went through with it.

"Damn, Dior. How in the hell are you still a virgin with a body like that?" Dream asked, smacking me playfully on the ass.

"I am not a fucking virgin. I had sex before…once."

"Oh hell no. Bitch, we definitely gotta get you laid out here. But you can't be an amateur out here, trying to take some big ass, ten-inch dick. You need to start off with at least a six and work your way up," Fantasy added as if she was some kind of expert on how to take dick.

"Shut up, Fan, and cut Dior some slack," Dream rolled her eyes in her sister's direction. "Don't worry about her, girl. With all that ass behind you, I can bet you my last dollar, some big dick baller is going to be all up in that shit tonight. Just be smart and make sure the nigga pays you well."

"Pays me? Ain't that some *Pretty Woman* shit? Sleeping with men for money?"

"Oh shit, I keep forgetting your country ass been out in Texas under her father's shadow, so you don't know shit about these niggas. We ain't got all night to give you the entire playbook, but we don't fuck with broke motherfuckers, okay? I'm not saying be a gold-digger, but just make sure if you're going to spread your legs, make sure that motherfucker is paid and he breaks you off decent. Your pussy has a price, baby, and if a nigga can't pay, he can't lay. This is all grade A shit over here, and trust me, if it's worth it, these niggas will spend them coins. But don't get it twisted, some will try and pull a quick one over on you, but you gotta be smart and know the type of nigga you're fucking with."

"Period, sister. And cousin, you're no stranger to money. Hell, your pops is rich as fuck, so you need to make sure the niggas you're fucking with can keep up with the lifestyle you're accustomed to back home. We ain't some cheap ass, broke, dumb bitches who are willing to fuck a nigga just 'cause he cute or he got on a platinum chain. If they want to take a dip in some sweet ass pussy, their pockets better be deeper than the Pacific Ocean."

"I got it," I said, double checking myself in the mirror. These two bitches may have been a little ratchet, but they were definitely about their money, and so was I. Seeing as how my daddy was getting tighter on a dollar these days, I needed to find a way to secure my own bag. And if I could catch a nigga who could match my daddy's pocket, I'd throw him all the pussy he could handle.

"Good. Now, let's roll, bitches. The money is waiting."

When we pulled up to the club, the line was stretched all the way around the building, but Dream and Fantasy headed straight to the front door as if they owned this bitch, and I followed suit. Dream gave the security guard a sexy smile and a kiss on the cheek, and without hesitation, he unhooked the velvet rope and let us straight through. This was how boss bitches rolled, and I liked that shit.

Hands down, we were the baddest bitches in this club, and as we stepped through, the crowd split like the Red Sea, making a way for us. By the time we made it to our VIP section, there was already a bottle of D'ussé and Patrón waiting for us. I wasted no time in taking a shot of Patrón to take get a little loose because I had plans on being tore the fuck up tonight.

All night long, the DJ had the club rocking, and we had our VIP section turned up. Everyone was trying to get in to party with us. We had niggas buying us bottles, throwing hundred-dollar bills, just to see us bend over in front of them. One nigga was so head over heels for Dream, he offered her a thousand dollars to let him eat her pussy in the middle of club. It was wild as fuck.

I had taken so many shots, my bladder was about to burst, so I had to find my way to the bathroom while Fantasy and Dream were busy snatching money. After I pissed and washed my hands, I reapplied my lipstick and slicked my edges back down with some water. Just as I was heading out of the door, my phone dinged with a text message from my dad. I hadn't even bothered to call him since I'd been in Tampa, so I knew he was probably freaking out. When I stepped out of the bathroom, I was busy trying to read my message when a familiar voice caught my attention.

"I thought I told you before about having your head down in your phone and not paying attention to where you're going."

I looked up to see that same rude ass motherfucker from the beach, standing in my face. He had this mean, dark ass look in his eyes as he stared back at me. I couldn't tell if he wanted to smack me down or grab me and kiss me. Either way, I got that same tightening feeling in my stomach, and my breath quickened when I looked into his eyes. It was something about the way his eyes held me in place that made my skin heat up and my mouth water. I strangely wanted to leap in his arms and tongue his cute ass down, but the thought escaped my mind as quickly as it entered once I remembered what a fucking douchebag he was. I pulled myself together, rolled my eyes at him, and attempted to walk away, but he grabbed me by the arm, pulling me back.

"Whoa, whoa, whoa. Where you going?"

"Away from your rude ass." I snatched my arm back with an attitude.

"That stank ass attitude of yours gonna get you fucked up one of these days."

"I got hands for niggas and bitches. I ain't never been scared."

"Oh yeah?" He glanced at me up and down, licking his full, pink lips. "I like that. Who you rolled up in here with?"

"Why?"

"Well, whoever you came here with, you need to tell them you leaving with me."

"Tsk. Nigga, you must be crazy. I ain't going nowhere with you, and even if I was stupid enough to say yes, that's not how you ask."

"Who said I was asking? But for real, though, go tell your peoples you leaving with me. I wanna talk to you."

"Talk to me about what?"

"Damn man, can you stop asking so many fucking questions? I ain't gon' hurt you."

I thought about it for a minute. My mind and body were begging for me to say yes as I parted my lips.

"I can't."

"Why not?" He inched closer towards me, backing me into

a corner. The closer he came to me, the more my airway became constricted. A mixture of alcohol, marijuana, and Creed cologne filled my nostrils as he pushed up on me. I couldn't escape it even if I tried — not that I wanted to.

"You scared of me?" His voice was slow and raspy like he was trying to hold his restraint.

"I'm not afraid of you."

"You should be. Come on, let's go." Grabbing ahold of my hands, he gently tugged for me to follow behind him.

"But what about my—"

"Shit, send your crew a text and let 'em know you with the mayor."

Something is Happening

Life

The second I saw that bitch from the beach earlier walking towards the bathroom, the very sight of her made my dick stiffen. I ain't ever been one to chase any bitch — I never had to — but it was something about this chick that had me feeling something different. I wanted her, and I wanted her bad. She had a slick ass mouth on her with stank ass attitude that both pissed me off and turned me on at the same time.

Being the nigga that ran this city, hoes threw more pussy at me than Brady threw touchdown passes. I could have any bitch I wanted in my bed, every single night, but most of these hoes didn't know how to act. You fuck 'em once and they think they're your main bitch. I was way too heavy in the streets to be tied down to one bitch, and I damn sure ain't need any more stress in my life. I had enough bullshit to deal with when it came to my son's mother, Angel. Every now and then, I would snatch one of these thirty thots up, dick 'em down real good, and throw their ass back to the streets. I ain't have time for love in my life; I was too focused on money. But for some strange ass reason, this little thick bitch was giving a nigga totally different vibe.

After I snatched her ass up out of the club before one of them broke ass niggas tried to spit game on her, I took her to this new hookah spot I was getting ready to open up in a few weeks. I didn't need a crowd of motherfuckers hanging around while I tried to get to know who this beautiful, sexy ass bitch was. We sat at the back table while I watched her blow smoke in the air from the hookah

I set up for her. This bitch was so fucking gorgeous, it was hard to focus on anything else but her all night.

"So, is this where you bring all your bitches after you force them to leave the club with you? Even the ones whose names you don't even know."

"I ain't force your ass to do shit. You wanted to be alone with me just as much I wanted your ass here, so don't play yourself."

"Do I get to know your name?"

"Life."

"Life? What kind of name is that?"

"That really ain't all that important."

"Well, Life, I'm Dior; you know, the dumb ass bitch who spilled your drink at the beach," she joked, blowing smoke in my direction.

I chuckled to myself. This bitch had some balls on her. She said whatever was on her mind, not even knowing who the fuck I really was. But I liked that, though.

"What you doing in my city?"

"It's spring break and my cousins asked me to come hang out with them. But in all honesty, I'm just looking for a nigga with a big ass dick to break my back all week."

"Oh, you like big dick ballers, huh?"

"You damn straight I do. And if you wasn't a rude ass motherfucker, I might've let you hit."

"Might?" I had to laugh that shit off. This bitch was clueless as to who she was fucking with. But then again, she wasn't from around here, so I had to give her a pass this time, but if she kept coming at me sideways, trying my gangsta, she was gon' see just what the fuck I was about.

"Trust me, if I wanted, I would have your thick ass bent over this fucking table, stuffing you with dick right now. Stop playing with me like I'm some weak ass nigga."

"Oh yeah?" She stood to her feet and walked in front of me. With lust crawling through her eyes, this bitch actually had the audacity to smack me in the face. "Do it then."

I didn't know if it was the liquid courage, or if she was really that bold, but either way, she'd just fucked up. Before I could stop myself, I'd jumped up and grabbed her by the throat, slamming her ass against the wall. It had been a long ass time since a bitch turned me on this bad. My heart was beating like a snare drum, and my entire body felt like it was on fire. This was a feeling I hadn't felt since I was with my hoe ass baby mama, before she fucked over a nigga.

The way her lips parted slightly, I couldn't help but lean in and kiss her. Kissing bitches was the one thing I never liked to do because it was too intimate, but there was this chemistry I felt with Dior that overpowered my senses. I couldn't think about anything else but being balls deep in her pussy. Our kisses intensified as my tongue danced around mouth, making my dick hard as steel. My hand tightened around her neck as I forcefully yanked her pants down. Pulling her G-string to the side, I caressed the slit of her pussy, and she was wetter than a motherfucker. As soon as I slipped my middle finger inside of her hole, her body tensed up instantly, and a soft moan escaped her mouth.

"Damn, you tight as fuck, bae."

"I want you to fuck me. Please, fuck me," she begged, tugging at my belt buckle.

Scooping her up, I laid her down on the table, ripping her pants off before pulling my shirt off and dropping my pants down to my ankles. I didn't have no rubber to put on, but right now, I didn't give a fuck. Finding her lips again, I kissed her passionately as I rubbed the head of my dick around her clit before attempting to stick it in but was met with resistance.

"Ahh." She cried out like I was hurting her, and that was

when I realized this bitch had never been touched before.

"You been talking all that big girl shit and you a fucking virgin?" I almost felt insulted a little bit. Something told me to stop right here and leave her inexperienced ass alone, but then again, I really wanted to break this bitch in and show her just how that slick ass mouth of her could get her into trouble.

"So what? I ain't scared to take dick. You gon' fuck me or not?" She caressed my dick before inserting it inside of her of hole.

Her pussy was so wet and tight, my dick felt like it was stuck in a vice grip, but it felt so fucking good. I tried to be gentle 'cause I knew my dick was way too big for her, but she talked big shit, so now it was time to see if she could take the D like a champ. Slowly sliding inside of her, that shit was so wet and tight, I had a hard ass time trying to focus and not bust prematurely.

"Aahh…ooohh, fuck. That dick so big, baby," she winced in pain, digging her nails in my back.

"Mm hmm. I thought you wasn't scared to take dick, bae."

"It's too big, daddy. Ooooh, shit."

"I know it is, bae." Holding her hips in place, I found her lips again, kissing her so tenderly before dragging my tongue across her jawbone until I was sucking on her earlobe. "I want you to take this dick for me, bae," I whispered in her ear. "You my lil' pretty bitch, ain't you?"

"Yesss, daddy."

"So quit, bitch, and take this dick." I picked up my pace just a little bit, rotating my hips as my dick slithered deeper inside of her wetness.

"Mmmh….Ahhh shit! You're gonna make me cum, daddy."

"Cum all on this dick, bitch. Don't hold back; let it go. Make a mess on this dick." Deep stroking that pussy, her legs began to shake, and her breathing quickened. I knew she was on the verge of busting a nut when I pulled out of her and dropped to my knees to catch her nut with my mouth. Eating pussy was something I hardly ever did 'cause these hoes didn't deserve that shit. Most of them was throwing pussy at half the niggas in the city anyway, so I wasn't about to put my mouth where another nigga's dick been. But when it came to Dior, she was pure. And the way she laid there and took all this dick, baby girl deserved some head.

Flicking my tongue rapidly on her clit while two of my fingers rotated inside of her, she cried out my name as she squirted her juices in my mouth. I instantly knew I'd just created a fucking headache for myself when I made her squirt. Most bitches had never had a nigga make them squirt, and if they found one, they became certifiable. But I really didn't even care at this point; Dior had a nigga head gone anyway, and I wasn't worried about her turning psycho on me. I was sure I could tame her thick ass.

Her body was convulsing from busting that nut, and she was whimpering like a new born baby, so I stood back to my feet, wrapped my arms around her waist, and held her tightly as I slipped my dick back inside of her.

"I know, bae, I know. It's okay, I got you. Just relax."

"Oh my God. That felt so good," she moaned.

"I knew you could take that dick like a big girl. Now, come here, I want you to sit on it." Keeping my dick buried inside of her, I picked her up and sat down as she straddled me. Lifting her lil' crop top over her big ass titties, I took my time sucking and nibbling back and forth on both of her erect nipples while her hips moved slowly in a circular motion.

"Mmmm, shit, daddy. This dick so fucking big."

"I love how you taking that shit. You so fucking sexy, bae." Grabbing her by the neck, I pulled her closer to me and kissed her soft ass lips, slipping my tongue in her mouth so she could taste her own juices. "Open your eyes and look at me while you riding this dick," I commanded and she obliged.

Caressing her back, my hands found their way to that fat ass, and I gave her a gentle smack every time she tried to close her eyes. I wanted her to look straight at me while she slid up and down on my pole.

"Didn't I say keep your eyes on me? Look at me while you riding me."

"Yesss, daddy. Ooooh fuck! You're going to make me cum again."

She was on the verge of busting another nut when I took over. Wrapping my arms around her waist, I held her still while I drilled my dick deep inside of her. Thrusting my hip up in a quickened pace, I forced her to keep her eyes on me as her juices flowed down my dick. I was quickly about to cum right after her when I realized I wasn't wearing a condom, so I hurriedly snatched my dick out just as my semen seeped out. Holding her in my arms as we both came down from that high, I couldn't believe how this bitch I barely knew had me feeling some type of way. If I was weak motherfucker, I would've been professing my love to her right now. But I had to admit, she damn sure had some fire ass pussy, and I was definitely feeling shorty. I wasn't trying to take this no further than right here, though. This was just my way of apologizing for the way I treated her at the beach, and now that we got that out of the way, shorty could go about her business.

You're Busted

Fantasy

It was going on seven o'clock in the morning, and Sage was just leaving the hotel room when Dior came tiptoeing through the front door. I could tell by the way the bitch was walking, like she was in labor or some shit, that she had got some dick. Last night at the club, she said she was going to the bathroom, and her ass never came back. Both me and Dream were so occupied with trying to score a big bag, I hadn't even given it a second thought who she was with or where she had slipped off to.

"You sneaky ass bitch," I called out, making her jump. "Where the fuck you been at all night?"

"Damn, Fan, you scared the shit out of me."

"I know I did. You wasn't expecting me to be hear, huh? How in the fuck you just leave us at the club and not tell us where you were going? I was close to calling the police and telling them your ass had been kidnapped," I lied. Even though I was happy to see her alive and well, I really just wanted the tea on who she was out fucking all night.

"I'm sorry. The nigga literally gave me no option. I meant to text you guys, but I got distracted."

"Obviously. So come on, sit down, and tell me what the fuck happened. I need all the juicy details, too. What's his name? Where he from? Is he fine? Was the dick good? Big or small? Did you get paid?"

"Okay, okay. I'll tell you, but first, let me order some coffee.

Bitch, my head is fucking killing me right now. My ass is still drunk ass fuck."

While we waited for the coffee to arrive, Dior changed out of her clothes and took a shower to get the stench of dick and semen off her ass. I laid across her bed, anxiously awaiting to hear what went down last night. She did say she was coming to Tampa for some big dick, and I guess she found it. I just wished Dream was here to get the scoop too, but she picked up some rich ass john last night, so she was somewhere securing the bag per usual.

After Dior finished showering, room service had brought up a nice ass breakfast for us to enjoy, but the only thing I was hungry for was some tea.

"So, spill it, bitch. What happened last night?"

"OMG, Fan, I think I'm in love. I know this was my first experience having sex, but that man made my body feel something I never could have imagined."

"Was it big?"

"Big ain't even the word. That shit was a fucking anaconda."

"So, who is he? How did you meet him?"

"Remember I was telling you about some rude ass motherfucker I accidently bumped into at the beach? Well, I bumped into him again when I was leaving the bathroom, only this time, he was a little nicer. Still rude as fuck, but nice. Fan, this nigga is so fucking fine, cousin. And his lips…" Closing her eyes and licking her lips, she laid there, replaying what this mystery man did to her.

"Okay. So, what else happened?"

"He took me to this lounge like place; it's not open yet, and he fucked the shit out of me. Fan, I know I'm an amateur, but this nigga had some good ass dick. The way he touched my body and kissed me so passionately; oooh, I was in heaven. And he put five stacks in my purse."

"Damn, cousin. You lucked up decent on that one. What's his name?"

"Life. And that's exactly what he gave me — life, bitch."

My heart damn near jumped out of my chest when that name slipped out of her mouth 'cause I knew this was not going to end well. Not only was Life possibly the most dangerous, ruthless motherfuckers to walk the streets of Tampa, he was the love of Dream's life. And once she got wind that her own cousin slept with him, shit was going to hit the fan.

Dream and Life used to fuck around with each other a while ago, but Life had a problem with commitment. Then, he found out how Dream made her living, and he wasn't with that shit. He broke things off with her, and my sister damn near lost her mind. She went Brandi from *A Thin Line Between Love and Hate* — stalking him, busting his windows out of his truck, and even claiming to have been pregnant by him. Life even had to put hands on her to make her stop her bullshit. Dream, on the other hand, just refused to let it go. She kept her distance for the most part because she knew how far to go test Life, but in her mind, he belonged to her.

"Fan? Fan? FANTASY? Bitch, snap out of it."

"Oh shit. My bad," I shook my head, trying to erase the massacre I just envisioned of when Dream got ahold of this information. "Bitch, you just threw me for a loop just now."

"Why? You know him? Damn, cuz, don't tell me I just fucked one of your exes."

"No, no, no. It's nothing like that. But if I were you, I'd tread very lightly with that nigga. Life ain't shit nice in these streets. That nigga is a cold-hearted savage."

"What does that mean? Like, he got a bunch of hoes on his tail or something?"

"No, this ain't got shit to do with hoes. Life is literally the king of Tampa and the biggest fucking drug dealer around. People love him and respect him because they fear him. You remember when we were kids and our pops used to make us watch that fake ass wrestling with The Rock and Stone Cold? And remember how everyone used to be scared as fuck of The Undertaker because he was powerful, fearless, and you just never knew where he would pop out from and send you straight to hell? That's Life. That nigga got more bodies than a fucking cemetery. He's the type of nigga you see coming and you run the opposite way. Ain't shit sweet about Life."

"Damn. I mean, when I bumped into him at the beach, he gave me this look like he wanted to rip my head off, and he was so disrespectful to me; he even called me a bitch. But last night when I saw him again at the club, he was still rude as fuck, but I took it as that's just who he is, and he doesn't necessarily mean any disrespect."

"Don't get it twisted. He ain't a bad dude in general, but he's just someone you never, ever want to cross. So, you really like him, or was it just some fling?"

"Honestly Fan, I wouldn't mind kicking it with him for the week, just because he's so fucking sexy. But with a nigga like him, I know he got plenty hoes, and I probably won't even hear from him again. Still, if we happen to run into each other again, and he wants to go for round two, I damn sure wouldn't be opposed to it. I'm just here to have fun."

"And fun we shall have. So, catch a couple Z's 'cause I know you ain't get none last night. Dream will be home later, and we're going to hit up this fire ass house party."

While Dior was in the room sleeping, I sat, nibbling on my fresh set of blinged out stiletto nails, anxiously waiting for the volcano to erupt, after Dream found out that she had some stiff competition when it came to Life. Even though I wished like hell my sister would just let this shit go with Life because he would never be with her again, I knew Dream all too well. While she may have been a beautiful ass girl on the outside, my sister was a bit deranged. She'd been on crazy pills since she was twelve years old, and for the most part, she held herself together, but when she was tested, the devil came out of her.

Dream was so fixated on getting Life back, she would do anything in this world to have him. I think that Life reminded Dream of our father. When he and Dream were together, he treated her like a queen; he was her protector. And when she lost him, she lost her fucking mind, and it took her a long time to snap back. Now that Dior had come and got her a piece of Life, I was terrified that Dream was going to go off the deep end, and she wouldn't be able to come back.

Shit Just Got Real

Life

"What's up with you, baby boy? How was school?"

"Good. I made a picture for you, Da Da."

"Oh yeah? Where is it? I wanna see."

Reaching in his Batman backpack, my son pulled out a piece of paper with stick figured family portrait drawn on it and held it up to the screen. At that point, I wished I could jump through the screen and wrap my arms around him and keep him close to me. Messiah was my one and only child, and I loved him more than anything in this world. He and his mother, Tiffany, lived in Atlanta, so I didn't get to see him as much as I wanted to, but I made sure to FaceTime him every single day. It broke my heart to not have my family in the same city as me, but the most important thing for me was my son's safety, and truthfully, I could sleep better at night knowing he was safe and protected far away from Tampa.

While I liked to think that anybody who knew me or even heard of me wasn't silly enough to come for my family, shit was changing in these streets and becoming more and more dangerous. Young, middle school ass motherfuckers who were trying to make a name for themselves would try and roll up on anybody just to climb up the ladder. These niggas ain't have no regard for human life, and that was scary. Messiah was my world, and if anything were to happen to him because some dumb motherfucker wanted to get at me, I would blow my own brains out. And when some pussy ass niggas rolled up on me one day and damn near succeeded at taking me and my son out, I had to get him away from here. The streets was the life I chose to live, not my family, and I just couldn't fathom losing my son because of my transgressions.

My baby mama, Tiffany, blamed me for almost getting our son killed and refused to let me see or talk to him for a while. I couldn't even be mad at shorty 'cause she was right. But there wasn't a soul alive that would ever deny me my rights as father. I never had a pops in my life growing up, and I turned to the streets for guidance; I couldn't let that be my son's outcome. So, I sat Tiffany down and told her straight up, she didn't ever have to say two words to me again, but I'd be damned if she didn't let me be a father to my child. Things still weren't peachy between us, but we had a mutual understanding, and as long as I was able to see my son's smiling face every day and I could fly up to visit him at least twice a month, that was all a nigga could ask for.

"Wow. That's beautiful, kid. You made that all by yourself or someone helped you?"

"No, me! I'm a big boy, daddy."

"Okay, excuse me. My bad, big boy. You know your daddy misses you, right? I love you so much, kid."

"Daddy, I wanna come with you."

"I want you to come with me too, baby boy. Maybe we can ask mommy and see what she says."

"Okay. I'm going to play with Batman now. Love you, daddy."

"I love you too, son. Always." Hearing my son tell me he wanted to come with me broke my heart and had me fighting back tears. There was nothing else in this world I wanted more than to wake up next to my son every single day, but as long as I was still in the streets, it would never happen. It was times like this when I thought about my life and if being in the streets was really worth me missing out on spending every waking moment with my kid. Yeah, I had money, power, and respect. I was taking care of my family, and they never had to worry about shit, and life was treating me incredibly well. But was all this shit worth it? What was it to have all the glitz, glam, money, cars, and hoes if my son had to grow up and not feel his daddy's presence every day? That kind of shit fucked with my mental heavily, but truth be told, the streets just wouldn't let me go.

"Y'all finish with your one-on-one session for the day?" Tiffany asked after Messiah threw his laptop down and ran off.

"Yeah, I guess he got more important shit to do."

"And what about you? You still got important shit to do?"

"What you mean?" I asked with a baffled look on my face, but I knew exactly what she was talking about.

"Don't play stupid with me, Life. You still running around in the streets?"

"I still got shit to handle. Bills gotta get paid, and I have a family depending on me. You expect me to just walk away from everything I worked hard for?"

"And what about Messiah, Life? Don't you think your son misses you? When are you going to grow up and leave that street alone before it takes you away from the people who love and need you?"

"Tiff, I hear you, but it's not that simple. It's hard to walk away from the only thing I've ever known. But I'm trying. I just want to be in my son's life. I want to be able to be a father without you hovering over me like I'm gonna let something happen to my baby."

"It ain't about whether you would let something happen to him intentionally, but living the life you live, how can you guarantee his safety? Don't forget all the bullshit you've done in your lifetime and how many people wanna see you dead. I refuse to let my son go down for your shit. So, until you can finally put your son first for once instead of chasing a bag and thot ass hoes, the only way you're going to be able to spend time with him is through this fucking iPad."

Before I could respond, she ended the FaceTime, and it was a damn good thing she did 'cause I was about to empty the whole clip on her ass. God knows I had a soft spot in my heart for Tiffany because she gave me the greatest gift in the world, but I fucking hated it when she snapped on me about Messiah. I knew she was right, and I couldn't argue with her about her reservations, but I just hated to hear the shit from her. I was hoping that since shit been running smooth around here lately, and motherfuckers weren't testing my gangster, making me act an ass, Tiffany would ease up and bring my son out to see me, but she wasn't having that shit.

Sitting my phone down on the desk, my whole mood went from sugar to shit after that conversation with Tiffany. I had actually woken up in a good ass mood today, especially after fucking that pretty ass thick bitch, Dior. My dick jumped every time I thought about her ass, and honestly, I was ready for some more. I'd never really been the type of nigga to be thirsty over any bitch; I'd usually dick them hoes down and dip on them. But it was something about Dior that put her in a category all by herself, and being the first nigga to ever hit that had me feeling some type of way. She gave me a feeling I just couldn't shake, and whether she knew it or not, she was about to be mine for spring break.

I poured me a glass of Hennessy and was just about to light up a blunt when a knock came at my door. My receptionist, Val, eased the door open, peeking to see if I was busy.

"Sorry to interrupt, Life, but you have a guest." Her sweet, innocent voice spoke as she smiled one of those sneaky smiles. Val was Bishop's godsister, and she'd just transferred from Central Florida to Tampa for school. As a favor to him, I agreed to let her run the front end of the funeral home, but I had to keep my eyes on her lil' young ass. More than just dead bodies were transported and stored here. I used this business to transport some of my biggest drug shipments without being detected, and I really didn't need no nosey ass bitches running up in here, stumbling on shit they didn't have no business.

"Who is it?"

"The baddest bitch you ever had on your team."

Val and I both turned our attention to Dream's crazy ass standing at my door. Today was not the day to be dealing with her bullshit. Tiffany had already pissed me off, and Dream was only about to fuck my day up even more. I nodded for Val to leave us alone so I could see what the fuck Dream was doing here. The quicker she said whatever the fuck was on her mind, the quicker I could get her ass up outta here.

"What's up, baby? How you been?"

"Cut the bullshit. The fuck you doing here, and what the fuck do you want?"

"Damn baby, why you so touchy? That better not be one of your little sluts you got working in here, either."

"Or what?"

"Or she'll be a permanently sleeping in one of these caskets."

"Man, whatever. What you want, Dream?"

"I miss you, baby. I miss us, and I want you back." She tried to grab my hand, but I snatched it away from her. Every single fucking day of my life I regretted fucking with this bitch. She was the main reason my heart turned cold, and I ain't wanna love a single soul no more. Dream was a beautiful ass girl, and I thought I could trust her with my life. I thought she would be the one I could share my life with, but that couldn't have been the furthest thing from the truth. Turns out, this bitch wasn't shit but a fucking gold-digging, pussy-popping, money hungry hoe who thought she could whip me with pussy and suck me dry. It was a damn shame she was so fucked up in the head 'cause I saw myself falling in love with her at one point. Now, all I saw was red every time my eyes landed on her 'cause I really wanted to kill this bitch.

"Fuck outta here with that bullshit, Dream. I ain't got time for this shit today."

"Come on, baby. You know I never meant to hurt you, Life. I've been begging for your forgiveness for years. When are you finally going to let it go? I love you."

"You don't love shit but money. Don't sit here in and my face and pretend like you ever gave a fuck about me. You saw me as a come up and played the fuck out of me. You really think I would ever give you another chance to fuck me over again? Bitch, you must me outta your fucking mind. You need to bounce the fuck outta my shit 'cause I ain't got shit else to say to you."

"What is the real reason you so upset with me, Life? Because I got rid of the baby or was it because I thought I could outhustle you? Baby, I told you million times, I had to find a way to survive in these streets after my daddy passed. It was up to me to figure out a way to take care of my sister and myself. All of that responsibility was on me, and I did what I had to do. But I also told you, if you wanted me to stop, I would've quit in a heartbeat if you would've married me, but you couldn't even do that."

"Bitch, are you high or something?" I looked back at Dream with pure hatred and disgust splattered across my face. This looney tune ass bitch actually had the audacity to sit across from me and try to justify what the fuck she did. Dream was the most certifiable bitch I'd ever come across, and I wished like hell I could reverse time and run like a motherfucker in the opposite direction the day I met her trifling ass.

"You really about to sit here and act like it was just about what you were out in these streets doing for money? You just gonna pretend like I ain't know you was fucking my own brother, and the baby you was pregnant with belonged to him? That's the real reason you got an abortion. But you thought I was motherfucking Boo Boo the Fool. Bitch, I got eyes and ears all across this motherfucking city. You was fucking Sage the whole time we were together, and you still fucking him now when you know your sister in love with him. Bitch, you ain't shit but a fucking dirty-foot ass hoe. As long as breath in my body, I'll never fuck with you again. Now, make this my last fucking time telling you to get the fuck outta my shit and stay the fuck away from me."

With tears and mascara running down her face, she knew better than to say another word to me. Instead, she stood up and took off running out the door like the building was on fire. I knew the things I said hurt her feelings, but I couldn't even find a fuck to give. Dream was as trifling and low down as they came, and I would rather chop my own dick off than to fuck with her again.

Downing my drink, I poured me a second shot and swallowed that in one gulp. That bitch had my blood on overboil, and I desperately needed to calm down. I really wanted to run after her and beat the fuck out of her ass for trying me, but I wasn't in the mood to go to jail tonight. I had to find another way to release all this pinned up frustration inside of me, ready to burst out, thanks to Tiffany and Dream. And I knew just the person I could call to help relax me — that thick ass Dior.

I was just about to hit her line when Bishop came walking through the door with a perplexed look on his face. Something was wrong. I swear, if he came at me with bad news, I was going to burst into flames. Today was just not my fucking day, but I was determined to make my night better once I got ahold of Dior. So, if Bishop didn't have nothing good to say, he was going to have to keep it to himself till tomorrow.

"I know that look, and whatever news you got, hold that shit off till tomorrow. My mind can't handle no more bullshit right now, or I just might lay a bitch down."

"Naw, Life, I can't do that. Listen man, I hate to fuck your day up ever worse, but I found out what the fuck happened the night Sage was jacked."

"Damn, nigga, you don't listen to shit. I said I don't wanna hear no fucking bad news."

"Man fuck that, Life! You need to hear it 'cause one of the motherfuckers who jacked your shit was the bitch that just ran up outta here. Her and her sister. And you wanna know the kicker? Motherfucking Sage set the whole shit up."

Feeling So Good

Dior

When I heard a knock at my hotel door, I double checked myself in the mirror, adjusting my breasts in my tight-fitting maxi dress. It was one of my favorite Valentino dresses because it hugged all of my curves and had my breasts sitting up perfectly. I quickly applied a bit of lip gloss to my lips and squirted Miss Dior, the only perfume I wore, behind my ears before running to open the door. Life was standing on the opposite side, looking fine as hell. My pussy instantly tightened, and I could feel the moisture forming as the corners of my lips turned up into a smile. I didn't even care to have any conversation at this point; all I wanted to do was get straight to business.

"Hey," I said lowly.

He looked me up and down, licking his lips before stepping towards me, swiftly snatching me up, throwing me against the wall. His lips found mine, kissing me hungrily while his tongue invaded my mouth, and his hands tugged at the straps of dress, forcing them down. From the way he was in a hurry to get me out of my clothes, I knew he wanted me badly, and the feeling was mutual. After he pulled my dress down, exposing my breasts, he created a wet line from my chin down to my neck, where he sucked like a vampire. His hands slid down my body, in between my legs, and began caressing my pussy. The thin material of my thong was already beginning to soak with my wetness, and the way his fingers rotated in a circular motion over my clit only aroused me more.

"That pussy gushing like a motherfucker. I want the fuck

out yo' thick ass," his ragged voice whispered in my ear while he continued massaging my clit with his fingers.

"I'm yours for the taking. You can do whatever you want to me."

Without hesitation, he cupped my ass, scooping me up and carried me to the bedroom and laid me down on my back. He stared at me with such hunger and intensity in his eyes as he quickly removed his shirt, leaving both of his thick Cuban links resting around his neck. Kicking his Retro 12s off and dropping his pants down, he leaned back on top of me, grabbing me by the throat and kissing me intensely. At this point, I just wanted him to stick it in me already, but all he was doing was teasing me with the tip of dick, moving up and down my slit.

"Stop playing with me, baby. Put it in me."

"That's what you want?" Guiding his dick to my opening, he rammed himself deep inside of me, making me gasp as his thick girth filled me up. Then, he snatched it right back out and stood tall.

"Lay flat on your stomach and suck my dick."

I obliged, doing just what he asked me to do. Never in my life had I ever sucked a real dick before, but I watched countless pornos and even bought a dildo to practice with. I wasn't sure just how good I would be, but for Life, I was willing to do anything for him. Opening my mouth wide and sticking my tongue out, I slowly moved my head halfway down his length before I started to gag and drool. Trying to suck a real dick was completely different from a plastic ass dildo. I felt like I was about to kill myself, trying to deep throat his massive dick.

"Come here. Open your mouth." Placing one hand on top of my head and the other under my chin, he slid his dick down my throat, keeping my head steady. I instantly started choking, but he didn't care. Thrusting his hips forward, he forced me to take all of him in as my mouth filled with saliva, wetting his dick up even more.

"Choke on that dick, bitch. Just like that. Look at me while you swallow that motherfucker."

Looking into his eyes while my mouth was stuffed with dick, turned me on like a motherfucker. I could see it in his eyes how bad he wanted me, like he was hungry as fuck for my body. Snatching his dick out, he laid back on the bed and pulled me on top of him. He held my hips in place as I slide down dick. My pussy was still recovering from the first beatdown he gave me, but I was still anxious for some more. Closing my eyes, I tried to adjust to his size, but Life wasn't trying to be patient or gentle. Gripping my waist, he held me tightly and began thrusting his hips upward. I swear, I felt his dick stroking all the way up to my chest — that's how deep he was inside of me.

"Hmm….oooh shit, baby," I moaned out.

"Ride this dick, bae. Fuck me like this your shit."

Planting my hands on my chest, I got on the tips of my toes and bounced up and down. I still couldn't quite adjust to the size of his big ass dick, but I was damn sure going to take that motherfucker like I'd been riding a horse's dick all my life. The more I bounced, the wetter my pussy became, soaking his shit up like I was pissing on him or something. I hadn't even been taking the dick for ten minutes before I was shaking and busting a nut.

"Oooh shit! Fuuuck, I'm cummin'! I'm cummin', daddy!"

"Don't stop. Keep fucking me. Make that pussy cum again."

"Mmmm, daddy! I-I-can't!" I cried out. "I-I-can't take anymore."

"Yes, you can. Stop playing with me, bitch. Keep fucking me till I feel that pussy cum again." Wrapping a hand around my neck, he squeezed me tightly, forcing me to continue bouncing up and down his shaft. The more he choked me and stared into my eyes with intense passion, the quicker another climax was rising inside of me. I could barely catch my breath as my entire body went into convulsions, and my juices flowed down his dick once again.

"Fuuuck! Fuuuck, daddy! Oooh shit!" He held me tightly as I cried out from another explosive nut. It felt like every ounce of energy was sucked out of me, and my body went limp as I collapsed on top of him.

"Umm hmm. That's a good girl. I knew you had it in you. Now, let me give you the grand finale." Flipping me over on my back, he hovered over me and guided my mouth open so he could slip his wet dick inside my mouth. "I want you to catch this nut, bae."

My head bobbed like a turtle going in and out of his shell until he busted his warm, thick cum in my mouth. His nut had a semi sweet taste to it as it slid down my throat. We were both so spent that all we could go was lay next to each other, trying to come down off that high.

I was waiting on him to get dressed and haul ass as soon as he caught his breath, but he didn't. Instead, he pulled me close to him so that my head was resting on his tattoo-covered chest. Five minutes hadn't even gone by before he was snoring softly, and I followed suit, closing my eyes with a smile on my face, enjoying the intimacy while it lasted. A satisfactory feeling came over me as I laid closed to Life, listening to his cute baby cow-like snores because I'd always heard women say that if you put a man straight to sleep after sex, you know you had some pussy. I guess my virgin ass pussy was snatching down there.

When I finally woke up, Life was still out like a light. I attempted to ease off of him to empty my full bladder, but as soon as I sat up, he pulled me back down.

"Where you going?" he asked with sleep thick in his voice.

"I gotta pee."

"Hurry back."

Sliding out of the bed, my hips felt like they had been locked for several days, and my pussy felt like someone used it as a punching bag. I was sore as fuck as I crept towards the bathroom, but I didn't even care. If having fire ass sex with Life meant walking like my back was broken for the remainder of this trip, I'd gladly attach a heating pad to my vagina and walk around on a walker like an eighty-year-old woman. After I finished peeing and making my way back to cuddle up next to Life, I had to stop and admire how fucking beautiful and sexy this man looked while he slept peacefully. Most of his entire upper body was nicely toned and covered in tattoos from his neck to just above his stomach. I noticed two portraits laying close to his heart, one on the left and the other to the right of a little baby and an older woman.

Crawling back next to him, I placed butterfly kisses from his belly button all the way up to his lips, where I pecked softly. He stirred a little bit before opening his eyes and smiling sweetly at me. Caressing the side of my face, he pulled me in a little closer for a deeper kiss, slipping his tongue in my mouth.

"You trying to go again?"

"I can go for hours with you," I replied. "But I was just admiring your tattoos. Who are the people you have right here?" I used a single digit to outline the faces of the portrait.

"My son and my grandmother."

"How sweet. I didn't even realize you were a father. How old is he?"

"Damn, you ask a lot of questions, you know that?"

"I'm just trying to get to know you a little bit, that's all."

"Trust me, the less you know, the better. I ain't really the type of nigga you wanna try and get to know. All this lovey dovey, having intimate conversations and shit ain't really me, ma."

"You took my virginity and just blew my fucking back out, but now we can't even have a conversation? It's not like I want you to tell me your life story. I just like you, and I think you like me too, but you wanna act all tough and shit. You don't have to be that way with me."

"It ain't an act. This is who the fuck I am. Don't get it twisted, I do kind of like you; you a pretty, thick ass bitch, but I just can't open myself up to people. It always gets me into trouble."

"What's with all the name calling? I been a bitch since I bumped into your rude ass a few days ago."

"My bad. I really don't mean no disrespect, but like I said before, I'm from the streets, and it's more like a term of endearment."

"Yeah well, I don't like that street term shit, so don't call me another bitch unless you stuffing me with dick, or you want me to fuck you up."

"Ha! You funny as fuck. But on a serious note, it ain't much to know about me, other than I'm a savage motherfucker. These streets belong to me, and I don't play about my family or my money. My grandmother raised me and my little cousin, but we're more like brothers. I have a son who I'd blow this whole world up about. Other than my family, my businesses, and my money, I really don't give a fuck about nothing else."

"What happened to your parents?"

"My mama died when I was kid, and I really don't know much about whoever my pops is."

"That's crazy. My mom passed away when I was a baby, too — cancer. I used to be super close to my daddy, but when he got remarried and had twins, I felt like I was replaced. I know for a fact that he loves me, but there's like a big void in my heart that I've been desperately trying to fill."

"Oh, so you a daddy's girl, huh?"

"I just want to be someone's girl. Just to know someone has my heart and shows that genuine love towards me, you know?"

"I feel you, ma. Shit, I honestly can't even believe you got a nigga laid up in the bed on some cuddle shit, doing all this pillow talk. But, if I'm gonna keep it G, I'm feeling you, and I fucking hate admitting that shit cause bitches—" He felt the way my eyes cut towards him when he said the B word yet again and quickly reverted. "I mean, women don't know how to act. Y'all tend to feel like y'all entitled, and that's some shit I don't fuck with."

"Well," I sat up and cradled his thighs, wrapping my arms his neck. "One thing about me that you need to learn quickly is that I'm nothing like these average bitches you're used to fucking with. And if you took a chance on me, you would see that."

"You gotta show me you're worth me taking a chance on, baby." Pulling me close to him, he found my lips and kissed me softly as he caressed my back. I could feel his dick getting stiffer as our tongues danced in each other's mouths, and I was definitely ready for round two until his phone started vibrating, interrupting the mood.

Grabbing it from the nightstand, he answered on the second ring.

"This shit better be important," he spoke between our kisses.

"You need to get to the house ASAP. Sage and his bitch waiting on you."

I overheard some deep voice in the receiver talking, and Life's entire mood switched. He didn't say another word to whoever it was that called him. He just hung up the phone and pushed me to the side. In a hurry, he started getting dressed while I was left sitting on the bed with a puddle between my legs, trying to figure out what the fuck just happened.

"You leaving? Is everything okay?"

"I got some shit I need to handle right now." He didn't even bother making eye contact with me as he slipped his shoes on and snatched his keys from the table. "I'm gon' fuck with you later, aight?" Giving me a quick peck on the lips, I couldn't even object to him leaving because before I could say his name, he was out the door. I honestly didn't really know what to think or how to feel, but all I did know was that Life gave me some type of feeling my mind and body had been yearning for, and I wasn't planning on leaving Tampa until I made him mine.

Life

Speeding down the highway, my mind was on one thing and one thing only — to keep my cool and not shoot the shit out of Sage and that thot ass bitch, Dream. Never in my life would I have ever imagined my own blood turning snake on me. But I guess this the type of shit good pussy made niggas do. Lord knows I didn't want to kill Sage, but if he didn't have a good explanation for the shit Bishop told me, he was gonna force my hand.

If nobody else knew me, Sage did. And he knew that snake shit was something I never fucked with, and I hated a disloyal motherfucker. Family or not, if a motherfucker crossed me or disrespected me on any level, my understanding was zero. Sage was one of the few people I trusted and let close to me. I raised the nigga from a little boy and taught him how to survive in the streets. What pissed me off was the fact that this nigga knew he could get anything in this world from me; all he had to do was just come to me. But I knew one thing for sure, if he was behind this bullshit with them bitches, he was no longer blood to me. He would just be another opp ass nigga in the streets, and the only way I dealt with an opp was to shoot that motherfucker in the face.

Pulling up to the restaurant, I was having all types of emotions zipping through my body. I didn't want to lose control of my temper, but I felt my blood begin to boil with each step I took towards the back room. The last thing I needed was my brother's blood on my hands, but I was prepared to handle business if Sage proved himself disloyal to me, especially over a scheming ass hoe. My patience had already run out with Dream's ass, on the other hand, so it was about time I laid her crazy ass to rest.

As soon as I walked inside the room, Bishop was standing in the corner with his gun out, and Sage was sitting tied to a chair, along with the bitch who was supposed to be Dream, but it turned out to be her twin sister, Fantasy. Even though they were identical twins, I could always point Dream out. Her eyes were slightly more slanted than Fantasy's, and she had fuller lips. But either way it went, I didn't give a fuck which twin it was; they were both guilty of stealing from me, so they would both pay the fucking price.

I could barely look at Sage because I was so fucking disgusted with his ass. More than pissed off, I was hurt that he could even be capable of setting this whole shit up just to get a couple dollars from me. I guess nowadays, loyalty to your family ain't mean shit to some niggas. Instead of hearing what Sage had to say first, I walked over to Bishop so he could tell me what the fuck was going on.

"This shit ain't looking too good, Life," Bishop spoke as we dapped each other up. I could see in his eyes that he was equally disappointed in Sage too.

"So, what's the word?"

"I found out that Sage never met up with Stan the night he claimed he was robbed. He had this bitch and her twin sister beat his ass and make it look like he was jacked, when the whole time, he planned this shit. This nigga been plotting on you with the same hoe you used to fuck with. I guess this was his way of getting you back for pulling her ass first."

"Oh yeah? That could be true, but that's not Dream; that's the other twin."

"So, this nigga been fucking both of them?"

"Sounds like it. But I do know one thing; I'm about to put an end to this shit." Walking over to Sage, my hands instantly curled up into closed fists. I was seconds away from knocking every tooth out of Sage's mouth, but I needed to hear from him why he would betray me like this.

"I only got one question for you, Sage. Is it true?" I stared at him intensely.

"Yeah, it is. I was tired of living in your shadow, always having to follow behind you and Bishop. Every nigga in Tampa think you the fucking Don around this bitch, and I'm just your fucking do-boy. I make more shit shake in these streets while you sit back and collect a check, only to give me what you think I deserve. Nigga, I helped build this shit standing right next to you, but instead of you treating me like an equal, you brushed me to the side. So, yeah, I took the fucking money 'cause I wanted to get the fuck away from you."

"I see. So, which twin was you planning on sharing the money with? Fantasy or Dream?"

"W-what? Dream ain't got nothing to do with this, Life. It was me and Sage's idea," Fantasy butted in.

"Hold up. Sage, you ain't tell Fantasy about you and Dream?"

"Shut the fuck up, Life!"

Before I even had the chance to think about my actions, I punched Sage so fucking hard in the face, I was sure I broke his fucking jaw. This bitch ass nigga had a lot of fucking nerve to talk crazy to me after stealing my shit, all over a hoe ass bitch.

"Nigga, watch your motherfucking mouth! Who the fuck you think you're talking to?"

"Life, don't kill him, please. We can get your money back, I swear."

"When it comes to this nigga, it ain't even about getting my money back. I couldn't care less about fifty stacks. I made three times that just a couple of hours ago. It's the nigga's betrayal over some pussy that's gonna get his bitch ass knocked off."

"I can give you back the money we took, Life. Just don't kill Sage. I'm pregnant with his baby." Fantasy continued to plead her case, but I wasn't hearing none of that bullshit.

"You pregnant by this nigga? Damn, Sage, you surprised me, bro. First, you go behind my back and fuck Dream and put a baby in her. Then, you go and do the same thing to her fucking twin? That's cold, bro."

"The fuck you talking about? Sage and Dream ain't ever sleep together."

"Oh, he ain't tell you that shit, huh? Aye, why don't you tell your bitch how you been fucking on her sister, little brother. Tell her how she ended up pregnant but got rid of the baby when she found out it wasn't mine."

"Sage, tell me this nigga's lying! Tell me you wasn't fucking my sister!"

Judging by the tears that began rolling down her face and the pain in her voice, I knew Fantasy was heartbroken. Not only was she betrayed by the nigga she fell in love with, but she also got played by her own fucking sister. I knew that shit had to hurt. And that nigga just sat there with the hush mouth, with nothing to say.

"I can't believe you would do this to me. I trusted you, Sage. I fucking loved you, but you went behind my back and fucked my sister?"

"It wasn't like that, bae." Sage could barely open his mouth to talk as blood dripped from his lips. I wanted to hit his bitch ass again, but I refrained. As far as I was concerned, I really didn't give a fuck about neither one of their sad tears and shattered hearts. They both stole from me, and they both had to answer for that shit. But instead of just shooting them in cold blood while they were both tied up, I figured I'd make Sage clean up his own mess.

"Yo, Bishop? Cut this nigga loose."

Bishop gave me a crazy look but didn't object to my request. Using a butcher's knife, he swiped the ropes confining Sage's arms and legs loose and jacked him up to his feet so the bitch ass nigga could look me in my eyes. Staring back at him, I no longer was looking at the same nigga I once called my little brother. This wasn't the same nigga who used to run behind me when we were little, trying to do everything I did. This wasn't my blood who I protected and took care of. As far as I was concerned, Sage was nothing more than an opp ass motherfucker who just crossed me in the worst way possible, and now this bitch boy was about to pay the ultimate price.

"Look me in my eyes and tell me, was this shit worth it? Was a few dollars and a piece of pussy worth you betraying me?"

"Bro, come on man. I'm sorry, aight? I messed up, but I'm sorry." He stood in front of me, shaking like a leaf on a tree. Looking into his eyes, I knew he was scared as fuck, but I didn't give a damn.

"Bro? Oh, now I'm bro? Was I bro when you stole from me? Was I bro when you chose pussy over family? Naw, I ain't your bro no more. You dead to me, bitch."

"I can get the money back, bro. I swear. D-d-don't kill me, Life. Please, man."

"Kill you? Naw, I ain't gonna kill you. But you gon' kill this bitch." Pulling out a gun from under my shirt, I placed it in Sage's hand. "You let this bitch get in your head to cross me, now take care of it. Or, I'll knock this bitch off myself and make you watch before I take your last breath, too."

"No, no, no, no, no. Life, please! Please don't kill me. I can get you your money. I promise, I can get your money!" Fantasy cried out.

"Bitch, shut the fuck up. It ain't even about the money. You should've thought about that before you coaxed my own blood into stealing from me. I ain't got no more wrap for either one of you motherfuckers. Sage, shoot this bitch, or I promise on my grandmother, nigga, you gon' die today."

"Life, please. Don't make me do this shit, bro. Please."

"I'ma count to five, and if this bitch ain't got a bullet in her, I'm gon' light your bitch ass up like some fireworks on the Fourth of July. Five…four…three…two…o —"

Before I could say the number one, Sage fired off two shots, hitting that hoe once in the chest and in the side. She screamed out in horror as her body slumped over.

When I looked over at Sage, who was whimpering like a pussy, weak ass bitch, this only added fuel to the fire running through my body. I hauled off and hit that bitch with a mean right hook, busting his nose till blood came gushing out like a running faucet.

"Nigga, how dare you stand right next to me and cry over a thot ass bitch? It wasn't enough that you betrayed me, but you got the fucking audacity to be heartbroken over this bitch." I stood over him and gave him a swift kick in the rib.

"I'm sorry, Life, damn! I didn't mean to fuck over you, bro! Come on, man. We blood. You my family."

"Family? Blood? Nigga, we ain't shit! You lied to me in my fucking face, and you let these hoes turn you against me. You can't come back from that shit, nigga." Picking up the gun off the ground, I held it right between Sage's eyes. The only thing stopping me from emptying the clip in that nigga's head was the vision of my granny's face flashing through my head. I knew if Sage wound up dead, it would break her heart, and to be honest, he deserved to walk around with the guilt of killing his bitch and knowing I was done with his ass for the rest of his fuck ass life.

"Life, don't do it! Please?! Please don't it, bro!" He begged for his life, and I would be lying if I said I didn't take pleasure in that shit.

"You know what, nigga? You ain't even worth it. The only reason I ain't gonna kill you is because of my grandmother. But just know this, if you ever even fucking think about crossing me again, I promise on my son's head, nigga, you gonna be a dead man." I attempted to walk away, but something evil came over me for a split second. It whispered and told me I needed to teach this nigga a lesson. So, I turned around and let off two shots, hitting that nigga in both his kneecaps.

"Make this your last time ever fucking playing with me, bitch ass nigga."

I dropped the gun and walked out of the room, leaving Sage yelling out in immense pain. I was angry that I had to hurry up and put as much distance between us before I ended up killing his ass. No nigga walking this earth had ever crossed me the way this nigga did and lived to tell the story. As God as my witness, I never wanted a nigga dead more than I wanted him dead. More than feeling angry, I was hurt that Sage, of all people, went against me, all for some pussy. This was the very reason I didn't trust no fucking body, and he proved me right once again. Not even family was loyal. I wasn't the type to display my feelings or allow motherfuckers to affect me in any way, but Sage fucked me up big time with this shit. I could feel tears sting at the back of my eyes, but I refused to let them fall. All this shit just made me close myself off even more. I could never let a single soul close enough to hurt or betray me like this again.

"Yo, Life? Hold up." Bishop came running out behind me just as I was about to get in my truck.

"What's up?"

"We got another problem. I just got a text from Quincy. He said his daughter is being held for ransom by her deranged cousin, and he wants you to find out who it is."

"What the fuck? How the fuck am I supposed to know who his fucking daughter is, and what this shit is all about?"

"You already know who his daughter is, bro. It's the bitch you been kicking it with. The one you bumped into at the beach that day. And you won't believe this; the bitch holding her for ransom is motherfucking Dream."

Me or Her

Dior

"Why are you doing this, Dream? What is wrong with you?"

"What's wrong with me? Bitch, are you really asking me what the fuck is wrong with me? You're what's wrong with me, bitch! You think you can just walk your big ass into my motherfucking city, fuck on my man, and think there won't be consequences? I don't think so."

"Your man? What are you even talking about?"

"Oh, bitch, don't act clueless. You thought I wouldn't find out you been secretly fucking Life behind my back?"

"Life? Are you fucking kidding me? Bitch, how was I supposed to know he was your man? It ain't like you made shit clear to me."

"Every fucking body knows that Life is my man! And since you wanna come to my city thinking just 'cause you're a spoiled, rich ass daddy's girl, you can just get whatever you want, huh? No, not this time, bitch. Life belongs to me."

"Oh, I see what this is all about. Bitch, you're jealous of me. You're jealous your so-called man fell for me. You're jealous of my life; jealous that I have money, I look better than you, and most of all, you're jealous I still have a father and you don't." I knew it was risky to toy with this deranged bitch's emotions, especially while she was pointing a loaded pistol at my head, but I really didn't give a fuck. But I obviously hit some major buttons because her already crazed eyes stretched even wider, and she slapped me as hard as she could across my face with her gun.

"You stupid bitch, didn't anybody tell you not to patronize someone with a gun in their hands? Hoe, you must want to die."

"So, you're going to kill me over a man?"

"Yes, I am, bitch, right after you get some of daddy's money to get my sister back. That dumb motherfucker Sage got her caught up in his scheming shit, and now Life has her. So, you're going to get your rich ass daddy to wire you $100,000 dollars, or I'm going to blow your fucking brains out."

"That won't be necessary."

We both looked to see Life standing at the doorway of my hotel room. Shortly after he left me here, this psycho bitch, Dream, somehow snuck into my room, attacked me, and had held me at gunpoint for the past two hours. She even made me call my dad to tell him she was using me for ransom to save Fantasy's life. I had no idea what all of this shit was about, until she finally confessed that she and Life had some sort of relationship going on that I had no clue about.

"So, you coming to this bitch's rescue? Huh? Where the fuck is my sister, Life?"

"First of all, watch who the fuck you raising your voice at. Second of all, you wasn't so concerned about your sister when you was fucking Sage, now were you? Now if you want to calm your ass down and talk like you got some sense, we can do that, but take that motherfucking gun off Dior's head."

"Why? 'Cause you'd rather be with her than me? Is that it?" Dream's voice began to shake a little. I almost wanted to feel sorry for her ass a little bit, but this hoe was certifiable.

"I don't want to be with that bitch. But trust me when I tell you, Dream, you don't want to fuck with me or her father. I can promise you on my life, you definitely won't like the outcome."

"Wait a minute. How do you know my father?" I asked with a

perplexed look on my face. I never once mentioned to him who my father was, and there was no way in hell he'd ever be involved with someone like Life.

"That's not important," Life waved me off. "Dream, look at me and listen to me carefully; what happened between me and Dior was nothing. It was nothing more than meaningless sex. But how can you expect us to be together if you hurt your cousin? Come on, now, you gotta be smarter than that shit."

"I don't want to hurt her, Life. I just want my sister, and I want to be with you."

"So come to me then. Let Dior go, and I promise you, I got you. We can make this work."

Like a simple ass bitch, Dream fed right into Life's sweet nothings. I could look in his eyes and tell he didn't mean none of the shit he said. Maybe he was doing it to save my life. I didn't know, and I really didn't give a fuck. All I wanted was to get the fuck away from all these crazy motherfuckers and take my ass back home to Houston. This had quickly turned into the spring break from hell, and I was so over this shit. For as long as I'd lived, I never wanted to come back to this city again.

As soon as Dream got within Life's arm's reach, he reached back and knocked her ass out with a mean left hook that she never saw coming. She hit the ground so hard, her head bounced off the floor like a basketball. Grabbing her gun, he stuffed it in his jeans.

"Bishop! Get in here!" he yelled as a big black, bouncer looking man entered the room. "Take her back to the restaurant and make sure the gun is in her hands when 12 get there."

"I got you, bro. You straight on everything else?" he asked, shifting his eyes to me then back to Life.

"Yeah, I got this." Once the room was clear, Life pulled out his phone and placed a call to who I was assuming was my father.

"I got her. She's okay, just a few bruises, but she'll live," he spoke into the receiver as he walked towards the bathroom and came back with a wet towel.

"Let me clean your face." He kneeled in front of me to wipe off the blood from my nose and cheek, where that crazy bitch hit me with her gun.

"How do you know my father?" I asked.

"That's some shit you need to holla at your ole man about, baby."

"But I'm asking you. First, you fuck me without telling me that you and my cousin had something going on, and now you don't want to tell me how you're connected to my own father?"

"'Cause it ain't your fucking business, aight? And for the record, I ain't know you and that dumb ass hoe were even related."

"Yeah, whatever." I didn't even want to look at Life, let alone have him touch me. I knew from the gate, messing around with a nigga like Life was a dangerous game. But against my better judgement, I let him get too close to me. I didn't want to catch feelings for him. I didn't want to even like him. All I wanted was a week full of fun, but when it came to Life, he opened up something deeper inside of me, something I couldn't shake. I was angry at myself for falling for a gangster like Life, but to be totally honest, in my heart, I knew I wasn't ready to just walk away.

"All that attitude is for the birds, ma. You knew what this shit was from the beginning, right? So don't act like I tried to play you or some shit. You came down here looking for dick, and dick is what you got."

"That's how you feel, for real? All this was for you was just sex? That's it?" I tried hard to fight back the tears because I refused to cry in front of this motherfucker. It was hard enough trying not to let my emotions show, but my feelings were hurt.

"It is what it is. But trust me, it's for the best that you leave and we never see each other again anyway. You and I come from two different worlds. You ain't built to handle a motherfucker like me, and I can't trust a bitch like you. I had fun with you, but this shit ends here. You got a private jet waiting for you first thing in the morning, so I suggest you get your shit together and go back to your spoiled ass, suburban lifestyle."

Life left me in my hotel room with my heart broken into shambles. Tears streamed down my face because I was so disappointed that allowed myself to fall in his trap. I should have known better than to ever think I would have room in Life's chaotic lifestyle. He only saw me as another notch on his belt, nothing more. It definitely hurt, but this was just the way the cookie crumbled when you dealt with a street gangster.

The next morning, my daddy called to tell me he had a car waiting to take me to a private airstrip to take a jet back home. I was happy to be getting out of here, but I was still taken aback by Life's reaction towards me last night. I tried to snap out of it, but I just couldn't shake the feeling I felt when we were together. But I knew eventually once I made it back home, things would get better.

After I boarded the jet and waited for takeoff, my phone dinged, signaling that I had a text message. When I opened it, I saw Life's name in the display box. Something told me not to open it, but curiosity got the best of me.

I owe you an apology for how all this shit played out. Just understand that I'm not the nigga you want to fuck with. You're beautiful and sexy as fuck, but I just can't let you get close enough to hurt me. Too many motherfuckers who claimed to be loyal all turned out to be snakes. I just don't want to hurt you. Just know that I fuck with you the long way, but a Tampa gangster ain't no good for you. Enjoy your life, ma.

I wanted to reply, but I didn't. I blocked his number, turned off my phone, and closed my eyes, preparing for my flight back home. This was one spring break I would never forget.

Join Our Mailing List:

http://eepurl.com/gU81k5

TMP
TANN MARIE PRESENTS
is now accepting submissions in the following genres
URBAN FICTION * URBAN ROMANCE
STREET LIT * URBAN PARANORMAL
INTERRACIAL ROMANCE
for consideration, please email the first 5 chapters of your manuscript to:
TANNMARIESUBS@GMAIL.COM

www.ingramcontent.com/pod-product-compliance
Lightning Source LLC
Chambersburg PA
CBHW072110150726
47999CB00005B/1973